The Bigger Picture

Forty Friendly Fables

Petrus Ursem

Forty Friendly Fables

Also by Petrus Ursem

THE STEVEN HONEST TRILOGY:
The Fortune of the Seventh Stone (part I)
The Truth Teller (part II)
Black as Ink (part III)

First published in the UK in 2022
by Gresham House Studios Ltd.
Gresham House, Cornwall, PL18 9AB
www.greshamhousestudios.co.uk

ISBN: 978-0-9955717-4-7

Cover design and all illustrations by Peter Ursem

1   Feeding Your Family

Blackbird was up early, as usual, and already hopping around on the lawn. He had this special technique of making some quick hops in succession, which he knew would, in the earth below him, sound like gentle thumping, like rain in fact. He then stood still and tilted his head slightly, listening closely with his better ear. In this manner he went around the lawn to wake up the earthworms, to hear them making their way to the surface, and be there — at the ready — when they would least expect it. Ah, there it was: the sound of moving earth that he'd been listening out for. Now, all set for the peck...

'Stop!' shouted the purple worm that had just popped up with wide open eyes and a furious roar resonating in his throat.

Blackbird stopped in surprise. Worms normally never had time to speak before he got them.

'Why?' he said. 'I need to feed my family.'

'That's fair enough,' said Worm, 'but forgive me when I ask if you can't see that you're being rather stupid.'

'What's stupid about feeding your family?' asked Blackbird.

'Feeding your family isn't stupid at all,' said Worm. 'Nobody in their right mind would hold that against you. It's the way you go about it.'

'What do you mean?' said Blackbird. 'Don't you think I'm rather clever, making you all think that I am rain, so that you wake up, one by one, and make your way, voluntarily, to my dinner plate? Wouldn't you say it's you lot who are the stupid ones?'

'Don't be daft,' said Worm. 'Do you really believe that we all think that you are rain, that we are fooled by your silly little hopping noises?'

'Well, why else would you come up to the surface when I hop around on the lawn?' said Blackbird.

'If you want to know the truth,' said Worm, 'it's because we pity you. We know you have a family to feed, and we also know that it's our duty to fill your plate. We're just humble earthworms, you see, not very important like you, and therefore willing and pleased to serve you as a meal.'

'Then, why did you just stop me pecking you up?' said Blackbird.

'Because there's a much better way, sleepy head!' said Worm. 'You see, what will happen if you eat me now is that all my six children in my home down below will not get fed today. So, they will die of hunger. And you know what that means, don't you?'

'What does that mean?' said Blackbird, slightly embarrassed to have to ask.

'It means,' said Worm, 'that today us worms may be plenty, but tomorrow we will be sparse. It means that tomorrow you will have to work just as hard, if not harder, to put food on your plate.'

Blackbird now looked thoughtful.

'You see,' said Worm, 'food stocks need to be managed carefully. If you eat me now, it means that there will be less for you to eat tomorrow. Whereas, if you could be a little less hasty and a little more forward thinking, my six children will have time to grow bigger and even start a family of their own. Soon there would be plenty of them to feed you and yours for many days and weeks to come.'

'I see what you mean,' said Blackbird.

Worm gave him a little more time to reflect on this and then said, 'Why don't you come back next week?'

'I'll do that, Worm,' said Blackbird. 'Thank you for your advice. It's very kind. I'll see you next week.'

'See you next week, friend,' said Worm.

And he popped himself back into the earth.

2   Says Who?

One day Bumblebee woke up with a bad headache. The headache was located right above her eyes and it felt like a constant pounding. Bumblebee tried to shake it off.

'I'll take breakfast and drink some water,' she decided. 'No doubt, it will soon subside.'

After breakfast she went to work as usual, but the headache kept hammering her forehead. While following her daily route, Bumblebee managed to forget about it for at least some of the time, concentrating instead on her business with flowers, but whenever her concentration drifted the headache was there, demanding attention.

Perhaps I should take some time off, she thought. Maybe a break would do me good.

The next day she stayed at home. She found it difficult, not doing anything, but — on reflection — she told herself that she had been pushing herself too hard, that she had been running her schedule too close to the edge and that she had no reason to feel guilty about taking a rest. She deserved it!

Regardless, the headache was with her for most of the day. Bumblebee understood that this was to be expected. After all, the headache had probably taken some time to build itself up and manifest itself so prominently and would therefore not suddenly disappear into thin air. And, secondly, the medicinal character of rest is that it will only work after a while, when — as it were — the levels of relaxation in the body would be sufficiently restored.

But when she woke up the next morning, the headache

still hadn't moved. Bumblebee felt this went too far. She wanted to get back to work. She missed smelling the flowers and was concerned, too, about letting their nectar go to waste. But how, being in this state, could she return to business? She decided to ask advice from her friend Bull.

'Bull, do you ever get a headache?'

'Never,' said Bull.

'Not even when you butt your head hard against a tree?'

'Not that I have noticed,' said Bull.

'But, surely, that must hurt,' Bumblebee tried once more.

'Not sure that it should,' replied Bull. 'I was designed to do that.'

Bumblebee wasn't getting any further here. Bull wasn't being helpful. You might as well argue that she was designed to be buzzing, but nevertheless this annoying headache had started bothering her. She flew off and decided to simply ignore the intruder in her head and try to catch up on the time she had already lost.

During most of the day she succeeded in ignoring the headache but when she came back home, later than usual, the pounding in her head was louder than ever.

'What do you want from me, Headache?' she shouted in desperation.

To her surprise there was an answer.

'Stop buzzing,' she heard.

'What?' said Bumblebee.

'Stop buzzing,' the Headache said again. 'Do you really need to be buzzing all the time?'

'But I'm a bumblebee,' said Bumblebee. 'Buzzing is

what bumblebees do! I was designed to buzz.'

'Says who?' replied the Headache. 'If you ask me, bumblebees should bumble, yes, but why should they buzz?'

'But I like buzzing,' said Bumblebee.

'Yes, I get that,' said the Headache, 'but you're not the only one here, are you? If you buzz all the time, I never get any sleep. Can't you be a little more considerate?'

Bumblebee thought about it.

'Everything in moderation would be a good thing,' the Headache added. 'We'd both benefit from that.'

They struck a deal. Bumblebee agreed she would buzz less, for example, only when she landed on a particularly sweet flower. The Headache was happy with this. It allowed him to slumber as he desired and thus leave Bumblebee in peace. In fact, the occasional buzz helped him turn over onto his other side and get comfortable again.

They tried it out for a week. Both felt it worked fine. Bumblebee even admitted that not buzzing constantly improved her sense and efficiency of smell. It made her better able to prioritise.

'Thanks, Headache,' she said, 'for letting me know.'

No answer came.

3　Being a Poet

'I think I want to become a poet,' said Moth to Owl.

They were both perching lazily on a rafter in the old barn, which had most of its roof missing. The summer day was turning its colours to dusk.

'Why?' said Owl, who had a reputation for asking clever questions.

'I just love words,' said Moth. 'I love to play with them, turn them upside down and inside out. I want to make them sing, because I love their sound. And their shape, too. I like how they feel in your mouth when you speak.'

Owl hadn't expected such a passionate and deep-felt outpouring.

'It sounds to me that you have what it takes,' she said. 'Why wait?'

'Do you mean I should try to be a poet now?' asked Moth, with a blush colouring his cheeks.

'Not try to be a poet! Just be one!' said Owl. 'Why waste time? You may feel that the night is still young, but I assure you that it won't last long.'

She paused for a moment, giving herself and Moth a chance to enjoy her own incidental talent for rhyme.

'You see, Moth,' she then continued seriously, 'you never know what lies ahead of you. For all you know, you may run under a bus in the next minute, or get caught up in a whirlwind, or lose your marbles. In the grand scheme of things we have little control over what happens next. Fate is a thing that drops from the sky. All we can do is choose our direction and follow it as well as we can and for as long as we live. So why delay? Why wait until tomorrow if you can start today? You must live in the moment! If you want to be a poet, be one!'

'Do you really think I could be a poet?' asked Moth.

'If you can be one tomorrow, you can be one today,' Owl said, still a little short of breath after her previous proclamation, which, so she thought, she had made rather eloquently.

'Thanks Owl,' said Moth.

A couple of hours later, when darkness was lying deep and low over the world, Moth found himself on a branch of the old oak tree, looking up at the night sky.

'Hey Stars,' he called out proudly, 'I'm a poet. What do you think of this?'

And he recited:

The night is young, my heart is free
The moon smiles at me, so wonderfully.

'Interesting,' said the Stars. 'A little clunky, perhaps. Might need to be worked on.'

Moth thought in silence for a couple of minutes.

'So what about this one, then?' he said, and he started again:

The day is done, the night is here
The birds find comfort on their nests
Yet, I long for the moon to appear.

'Mmm,' said the Stars. 'Better, but maybe a touch too sentimental? And what about us?'

Moth took another pause for thought.

After a while he said, 'I think I've nailed it now. Listen to this:'

The summer night embraces me
All is right, nothing's wrong -
The moon and stars all sing my song.

'Perfect!' the Stars said. Out of pure joy they regrouped themselves into the sheet music for a jolly tune, to be sung instantly by anyone who could read music. Owl, still in the old barn, observed it calmly.

Someone, somewhere, must have had some proper inspiration, she said to herself.

4   Hedgehog

For the twelfth time Hedgehog rolled over onto her other side. Or was it the thirteenth time? What was the matter with her? Why couldn't she get comfortable and sleep? It wasn't usually an issue — closing the door on a productive night, letting her eyelids go heavy, whilst somewhere beyond her den the sun stretched its first rays into the sky of a new day. At least, it never had been a problem — until now. What was keeping her awake? She had fluffed up her pillows, several times already, and she had checked and double-checked that all her spines had folded in correctly. Not a single one was sticking out awkwardly and creating discomfort. It had to be something on her mind that kept her from sleep, some kind of mental obstruction. She had tried a couple of the old tricks for dozing off, like counting sheep or thinking of words beginning with the letters of the alphabet in reverse order, but neither had worked. Her mind stayed in gear and her eyes wide open. Her whole being remained alert and as bright as a button.

As consciously switching off seemed unachievable today, she thought she might as well go the other way and purposefully re-engage her brain cells, either to work out what was wrong or, in any case, not waste the waking hours. In her mind she went over the various to-do lists she kept, but she couldn't find any outstanding issues or late completions. Food and foraging were hunky-dory, her stomach currently nicely round and her storage cabinets stuffed equally full. Housekeeping? The den wasn't due another dusting for at least three days, insulation was in good nick (she had checked before she went out last night), and that there was a healthy stream of fresh air, whilst the blinds and soundproofing worked to perfection, could be determined right here and now, as she lay in the quiet, sweet-smelling darkness of her home. Social engagements, then? She had sent the birthday card to Frog and the upcoming masked ball was definitely firmly in her mind, too. No, as far as she could tell, everything important was under control and up to date. The past night hadn't even been particularly eventful. Nothing out of the ordinary, she thought. So why didn't she just drop off?

She remembered that she had bumped into Jay, soon after she had left home. Jay was a funny character, never unfriendly, although you weren't always completely sure what he really thought about things.

'Evening, Hedgehog,' Jay had said. 'At it again? Sticking to your well-trodden path?'

Hedgehog now wondered whether Jay had meant that as a compliment for working hard and keeping her usual route well maintained, or whether he had in fact been critical and, with a dose of sarcasm, mocked her for always doing the same. But such thoughts always came much later; now, in fact, as she was lying here, recalling the meeting. At the moment itself, Hedgehog was never quick enough off the mark to retort with something witty. So, she had simply answered Jay with, 'Good evening, Jay. Yes, absolutely, one likes to know where one is heading.'

'Yes, don't we all?' Jay had said. 'As for I, my bed is waiting. Bidding you a productive night, Hedgehog.'

And he had flown off, shooting into the forest with a

blue flash of his special feathers.

Hedgehog wondered why Jay always said 'I' instead of 'me'. Perhaps it made him feel more important.

Half an hour later Hedgehog had literally walked into Crocs, who was pacing up and down along the beech trees.

'I'm terribly sorry,' Hedgehog said. 'I hadn't expected to see anyone here at this time of night and I didn't look where I was going.'

'My fault, completely,' said Crocs, quickly showing that famous broad smile on his face. 'I'm being erratic. Should pay more attention.'

Hedgehog could tell that Crocs was not his usual warm-hearted, jovial self; that his swift smile still bore traces of an earlier frown.

'I hope I haven't unwittingly disturbed you in your affairs?'

'Not at all,' Crocs said. 'Always good to see a friendly face. I was just going over my material for the final, that's all. You probably know about it, don't you, that I'll be facing Frog in the last round? I want to strike the right balance, you see, given the times we're in.'

'Certainly,' Hedgehog said. 'Don't let me distract you. I'm looking forward to it.'

She had quickly shuffled on. Of course, she knew about the forthcoming quiz final between Frog and Crocs. But wasn't that still some time away?

For the next couple of hours Hedgehog had continued without further distractions, but then she spotted Owl and Moth on the lower branch of the old Oak. It sounded as if they were having an argument.

'That's not at all what I'm saying,' she heard Moth say.

'You're twisting my words.'

'Not my intention,' Owl replied. 'My apologies. I'm just trying to understand the core of the matter.'

'Well, I can't say it any other way,' Moth said. 'I know it's complicated, but you have to grant me poetic licence. I have considered my words very carefully.'

'Naturally,' Owl replied. 'Far be it from me to doubt your skill with words and your understanding of their deeper meaning in any sense or form, and please ignore my thoughts if they're of no use to you. I'm only trying to be the voice of reason here. It's just that I'm concerned that not everyone will be able to pick up the finer nuances in your eloquent turn of phrase. After all, you are our cherished poet and I wouldn't want you to be misunderstood.'

Hedgehog had no idea what exactly they were talking about, but Moth and Owl were so deeply engaged in their exchange that they didn't even notice her down on the ground. She didn't like to be eavesdropping, so she had moved on before they could catch sight of her.

And now, as she lay in her den, recalling the night's encounters, she thought about how different everybody was: Jay, with his ambiguous way of speaking; Crocs, performer through and through, and ever aware of what impression to make; Moth and Owl, each in their own way burning a candle for truth. It seemed that they all had a special talent, be it Moth's poetry or Owl's logic, or being able to mock like Jay or win hearts like Crocs. None of them was taken up with daily routines, like she was. They all had their minds set on other matters, on things of a higher order perhaps, things above and beyond the here and now.

All of a sudden, a hot feeling took hold of her. Had she been ignorant and naive, she asked herself. Given the times we're in, Crocs had said. What had Crocs meant? Was she, Hedgehog, missing something? Was she wasting her time on trivial business, unaware of the bigger scheme of things? Shouldn't she be nurturing a talent, if, at least, she could first work out what her talent was?

Needless to say that all desire for sleep she might have had remained unfulfilled. All day long, as outside her den the sun carved its curve through the blue sky, Hedgehog lay restless, thinking about how she could be more special, what gift she might find in herself that would make the others notice her more, and perhaps even earn their respect. She was glad when, at last, dusk arrived, telling her it was time to get busy again.

5 Seeing Beyond

Fish was having a good time, or so it seemed, because she was jumping up and over the water. The sun was shining and wherever Fish caused a stir the river surface exploded like a firework of brilliant twinkles.

Frog, who had been observing the spectacle for some time, called out to Fish.

'You're joyful today, Fish, jumping about like that. What makes you so happy?'

'I'm always happy,' said Fish, 'but not so much today. I'm trying to see beyond the horizon, but I can't get high enough. Can you see anything from where you are?'

'I can see the horizon,' said Frog, 'but I can't see beyond. Wait, let me try this.'

He bent his knees and projected himself as high up into the sky as possible, landing with a thud back onto his lily pad.

'No, I can still only see the horizon,' he said. 'I can't see over it.'

'What a nuisance,' said Fish. 'I so want to know what lies beyond. How can we find out?'

'Let's ask Squirrel,' said Frog. 'He could climb to the top of the highest tree for us.'

They went to find Squirrel.

'Will you do us a favour?' asked Fish. 'We're trying to find out what is over the horizon. Will you go up in the trees and tell us what you can see from there?'

'No problem,' Squirrel said.

He disappeared in between leaves and branches, only occasionally showing the red of his tail, but he was back soon enough.

'I'm sorry, friends,' he said. 'I went as high as I could. Up there you can see the horizon clearly, but I couldn't see what comes next. You'd need to go up even higher, I think. Perhaps we could ask Bumblebee.'

The three of them looked out for Bumblebee.

'Bumblebee, we need your help,' said Frog. 'None of us can jump or climb high enough to see over the horizon. Would you mind flying up into the sky and letting us know what lies beyond?'

'Sure, I'll give it a go,' said Bumblebee.

Fish, Frog and Squirrel waited patiently for her return.

'She should be able to do it,' said Squirrel. 'After all, Bumblebee isn't earth-bound, like we are. I sometimes feel as if I could fly but without wings it would be unwise to really let go.'

Ten minutes later Bumblebee was back.

'I hate to disappoint you,' she said, dashing their hopes. 'It's too cold for me. I went up as high as I dared, more than three times my normal altitude, but I still couldn't see over the horizon. With my type of wings it's too risky to go any higher. Why don't we ask Eagle?'

When they saw Eagle circling above them, they called her down.

'Sorry to bother you, Eagle', said Fish. 'We need to know what lies beyond the horizon. You have better eyes and stronger wings than any of us. Will you fly to the end of the sky and find out what you can see from there?'

'Of course, I'm happy to help,' said Eagle.

She set off immediately, soon became a tiny dot in the vast expanse of sky, and then disappeared completely. More than half an hour went by before she returned.

'I'm so very sorry to bring disappointing news,' Eagle said. 'I don't think I've ever been that far and that high. I could see a lot, and it certainly seemed that there was something there, beyond the horizon, but, as much as I tried, I couldn't get closer, and I really wasn't able to tell what it was. The best I can suggest is that we ask the Stars.'

So, the five of them waited until the sun started setting, the skies darkened and the Stars lit up, one by one.

All at once they called out to them.

'Stars, what can you see beyond the horizon?'

'We'd love to be able to tell you,' the Stars said, 'but it's too dark on that side to see clearly. You may have a better chance tomorrow, by daylight.'

It was difficult to hide their disappointment. They felt exhausted, too.

'Let's try again tomorrow,' suggested Frog.

What else could they do? They all went home and dreamed of what they might see beyond the horizon.

6   An Invitation

Ladybird had a special talent. She was exceptionally good at mathematics. No figure was too big for her, no calculation too complicated.

For example, Squirrel might visit and ask this question:

'If the winter lasts for ninety-five days, I eat seven nuts a day and three extra at weekends, and if the first day of the new harvest is eleven weeks into spring; how many nuts should I put into storage, taking into account that my winter supply may be affected by ten percent nut rot?'

Ladybird would give Squirrel the correct answer without even closing her eyes during the adding up.

Or, Bumblebee might want to know whether it would be better to harvest pollen from large flowers, so that there was less flying up and down to do, or whether she should instead frequent more small flowers and thus be able to fly with lighter loads. And what impact this may have on the quality of the mix.

In response to that type of question, Ladybird would clearly summarise both scenarios, detailing the pros and cons with measurable figures, thus enabling Bumblebee to make an informed choice. Ladybird's sharp talent for sums brought clarity to some of the essential questions in life, and many animals would eagerly seek her advice on the best cause of action in a particular situation.

Ladybird used her talent to her own benefit, too. For example, she had put together detailed charts of the average weather conditions in various locations, allowing her, by statistical deduction, to avoid rain on her travels. In secret, she also kept mood charts of her contemporaries, based on detailed behavioural observations. These mood charts enabled her to determine, precisely to the minute, the best time to ask someone for a favour or make a proposal.

Yet, no matter how impressive Ladybird's calculated wisdom was, she could not solve all the mysteries in the world, because one day, out of the blue, she received an invitation in the post that she had not foreseen. It had a beautiful golden border printed around the edges, but it wasn't signed. It simply said:

'Please meet me tomorrow night at eight in Chestnut Lane for a candlelit supper.'

Ladybird had no idea who the sender might be. There was a hint of romance in the phrasing of the invitation but she couldn't think of anyone with that kind of interest in her. She consulted her mood charts but they gave her no answer, as at least twenty entries were capable of unregulated or romantic outbursts. With regard to this enigma, she really didn't have a clue and that annoyed her. She considered, of course, ignoring the invitation, but she then concluded that accepting it was probably a more efficient way to resolve the matter.

The next day was quiet. Moth was the only one who came to seek her help. It was on something simple: how many different words you can use before you have two that rhyme. Not all that difficult to work out!

In the evening Ladybird prepared herself for the supper invitation. By no means did she plan to immerse herself, just like that, in a romantic encounter with a mysterious character, but she felt it was wise, also, to at least be prepared. So, she brushed her frock and sprinkled herself modestly with a not too overwhelming perfume.

On the dot of eight she arrived in Chestnut Lane. Halfway down the lane a round table was set up and elegantly laid for supper. In the middle of it a candle burned with underneath it a note saying, 'Welcome, Ladybird, please sit down.'

As she did so, an orchestra started playing. Then, suddenly, all the animals jumped from behind the chestnut trees and started singing 'Happy Birthday'.

'But it's not my birthday,' protested Ladybird. Her mind quickly scanned through the pages of her diary — left at home — to check if she had, somehow, completely misread the calendar.

'Not your birthday, silly,' said Moth, who clearly was the cheerleader, 'but you have solved your thousandth problem today. That's why we're giving you a party; to thank you for all your brilliant advice over the years. You have helped every one of us with matters small or big, and you never asked for anything in return. So, tonight we just want to say thank you. Let the party begin!'

And so it did. All night long Ladybird, at her dining table, was served the most delicious snacks, while the orchestra was playing. Many came forward with an entertaining poem, act or song, remembering her mathematical achievements. Ladybird tried her hardest not to calculate how much all of this must have cost. For once, it didn't matter. It was the most splendid evening she'd had in a long time.

7   Being in Love

'Owl,' Goat said, one afternoon, 'what does being in love feel like?'

'Oh, well,' said Owl, 'that's hard to describe. Your stomach feels upset — queasy, that's the word I guess — and you go hot and cold at the same time, and it's difficult to concentrate on things.'

'Have you ever been in love, Owl?' asked Goat.

'Personally, I haven't,' said Owl.

'Then, how do you know what it really feels like?' said Goat.

'Well, you know,' said Owl, 'I listen to others talk about it. And I have read books and poetry, and such.'

'But no first-hand experience?' Goat insisted.

'No, as I said, not personally,' said Owl. 'Maybe go talk to Moth. He's a poet. He may be able to tell you more exactly what you want to hear.'

'Thanks, Owl,' said Goat.

Later that evening Moth came fluttering by. He was on his way to his favourite perch in the old oak tree. Goat called out to him.

'Hey, Moth, stop for a moment, if you please. May I ask you a question?'

'Of course,' said Moth, and made a U-turn back to Goat. 'Fire away.'

'Have you ever been in love, Moth?' asked Goat.

'Oh, yes, many times,' said Moth, 'but, unfortunately, always unsuccessfully.'

'How does it feel, being in love?' asked Goat.

'It's not very pleasant,' said Moth. 'It's a kind of

restlessness; a feeling as if you don't know if you want to stay where you are, or go somewhere else. And you feel hungry, but, at the same time, eating anything will make you feel sick. It's as if you are in a dream-world. Everything around you looks bright and colourful but, when you reach out to touch things, sometimes they're not even there. Being in love makes me very sad, too. Melancholic. As I said, it's not very pleasant. Mind you, it's good for writing poetry. One has to suffer for one's passions, I suppose.'

'How long does it last?' asked Goat.

'That depends on how seriously in love you are,' said Moth, getting ready to fly on again. 'Why? Are you in love?'

'I might be,' said Goat.

The next day Crocs dropped by. He gave Goat one of his famous broad smiles.

'Rumour has it that you're in love,' he said.

'Yes, I am,' said Goat, and he stared sadly into the distance.

'So, why so sad?' asked Crocs. 'Who's the lucky one? Or are we not allowed to know?'

'What do you mean?' said Goat.

'Well, who is it? Who are you in love with?'

'Nobody,' said Goat.

Crocs turned his smile into a look of surprise.

'What do you mean, nobody? Don't you want to tell me, or is your love not being answered?'

'I'm in love with nobody,' said Goat. 'I'm just in love.'

'But how can you be in love, if there's nobody to be

in love with?' Crocs asked.

'I just am,' said Goat. 'I have all the symptoms of being in love, so there can't be any doubt. I feel longing and I feel sick. I'm hungry, but I don't want to eat. I can't think of anything else. One moment I feel hot, but then, suddenly, I'm not. You see, I'm even speaking in rhyme.'

'I see, I understand it now,' said Crocs, full of pity for his friend. 'I'm very sorry to hear it.'

'Thank you,' said Goat.

They remained silent, just being together and feeling the feelings. After a while Crocs said, 'I tell you what. Why don't you just take it easy for the rest of the day? Just let it be, you know. Don't be too hard on yourself.'

'You think I should?' asked Goat.

'Absolutely!' Crocs said. 'These are complicated emotions. You can't just step over them. Have some me-time and perhaps, with some well-deserved rest, you will soon get yourself together again and start feeling better. If you would like it, I could pop round again tomorrow to see how you are?'

'Thanks, Crocs, that's grand of you,' said Goat.

'No problem,' said Crocs, and he beamed another warm-hearted smile at his friend.

8   Cyrus

'Good morning, Snake,' said Blackbird, 'and what a glorious morning it is, don't you think? It looks like a splendid day has come our way.'

'It's Cyrus, actually,' Snake said.

'Pardon?' said Blackbird. He looked at Snake, not understanding.

'It's Cyrus from now on,' said Snake. 'I wish to be known as Cyrus.'

'I see,' said Blackbird. 'Well, I must say that's a wonderful name, although it may take me a little time to get used to calling you Cyrus, Snake. May I ask; what's the reason for this change of identity?'

'It's not a change of identity,' said Snake. 'I was always Cyrus. It's just that you lot always chose to call me Snake instead.'

Snake's voice trembled, as if he struggled to contain a bucket full of anger, that must have been filling up inside him for quite a while. He seemed not at all to delight in the magic of the morning. And now, Blackbird's busy mind had to work hard to process all that Snake was letting out. Had they always done Snake an injustice by not calling him Cyrus? But how was anyone to know? Who did Snake have in mind when he said, 'you lot'? (Which, in Blackbird's view, sounded rather disrespectful). And, given that he had already slipped up just now, would he instantly be able to remember his friend's new name from now on?

'I'm so sorry,' Blackbird said. 'I guess we should have known. I'll do my best to remember that I should address you as Cyrus. Please forgive me if I forget accidentally, as I'm getting used to it. It would only be a matter of habit.'

'It's not that difficult, is it?' Snake said. 'Come on, say it.'

'Well, no, it's not difficult..., Cyrus...,' Blackbird said. 'I'll really try to get it right in the future. I guess it's just different, as we're all known by what we are, rather than having another name.'

'Not true,' Cyrus said. 'Crocs is called Crocs, isn't he?'

'But that's an exception,' Blackbird said. 'Besides, Crocs isn't really a different name; it's just an abbreviation.'

'Not an exception any longer,' Cyrus said. 'I don't get why you wish to argue the point. Is it such a big ask to just call me by the name I choose?'

Blackbird knew he was on thin ice and had to tread carefully.

'Of course not, no, yes, sure, Cyrus...' he said. 'Forgive me. Naturally, that is no problem at all. I didn't mean to argue against your wishes. I'm just trying to understand, given that I don't have the best memory for names. It was pure selfishness, I guess.'

'Mmm,' said Cyrus.

He seemed to relax a little.

'Fair enough. I can see you may need some time. But look at it from my point of view for a moment, if you don't mind. You and all the others — you've always called me Snake. But I'm not just a snake, am I? If you want to be precise, I'm a grass snake, actually. Not an adder or a boa constrictor, a grass snake. Yet, you've never called me that. You've always gone for Snake. That's the same as if I were to call you 'Bird', instead of Blackbird, or if I were to call Ladybird 'Insect' or Hedgehog 'Hog'. That would be somewhat insulting, wouldn't it?'

Blackbird had to admit Cyrus had a point. He couldn't imagine ever wanting to call Hedgehog 'Hog', or Ladybird 'Insect', and he definitely didn't like the idea of anyone calling him 'Bird'. On the other hand, Owl was just Owl and Fish was just Fish. But Blackbird wisely chose not to make any counter arguments this time.

'I wish to be known for who I am, not for what I am,' Cyrus said. 'Grass Snake is rather a mouthful and sounds a tad pedantic. Cyrus is more precise and fits perfectly with who I am. So, if you don't mind...'

'Sure,' Blackbird said. 'I mean, absolutely. I agree. Cyrus is a good name, and there's nothing wrong with making a new start.'

'Excellent,' Cyrus said. 'That's settled then.'

He now looked a lot more relaxed.

'So, shall we?'

Blackbird looked at his friend, again not understanding what he meant.

'Make a new start,' Cyrus helped.

'Of course,' Blackbird said. 'Forgive me, I'm slow off the mark again.'

And then he said, 'Good morning, Cyrus, and what a glorious morning it is, don't you think? It looks like a splendid day is has come our way.'

'Absolutely,' Cyrus said. 'If every day would start like this, I say, bring it on. Isn't it wonderful to be alive?'

'It certainly is, Cyrus,' Blackbird said.

9   Being Fed Up

Bull was fed up. It had been raining all week long and his favourite field had been turned into a terribly muddy patch. No, he didn't mind a bit of wet, and he didn't mind a splash of mud, but after a whole week of rain he was soaked to his skin. He felt that enough was enough and called up to the clouds.

'Can't you make an end to it? I've had enough rain on my back now, thank you.'

But nothing changed, up there. Above him the clouds remained an indifferent, solid formation of greys and blacks, sliding through the sky as a tightly woven, sombre cloth.

Bull decided to ask Owl for advice. He realised, of course, that the natural elements are a force in the world that we mortals have little influence over, at least, not in the short term, but with Owl you never knew. Everyone said she was full of clever tricks and wisdom.

'Owl,' said Bull, 'what should one do when one has had enough?'

'Enough of what?' Owl wanted to know.

'Well, enough of that rain for example,' said Bull. 'It has been coming down relentlessly for a week now, and I just don't see why I should put up with it any longer.'

'I fully and utterly agree with you,' said Owl. 'The question is: what can be done about it? You see, normally, when one is put in a situation that is unacceptable and unreasonable, my advice would be to go on strike. However, the problem here is that we don't even know who or what is causing this situation.'

'What is 'going on strike'?' asked Bull.

'It means that you stop doing something that you are supposed to do, like talking or eating or sleeping, simply to force the other party to listen to your concerns and take you more seriously. You need to do it very visibly, making sure that they can't ignore you. For example, you stop talking in broad daylight. Or, you stop sleeping, but not in your bed, in the middle of the street. And you mustn't stop doing those things on your own, but you must stop doing them with as many as are willing, to show that, together, you have a strong voice. The other party and everyone else must be able to see clearly that you all have extremely good reasons not to be doing what you are supposed to be doing.'

'That's an interesting notion,' said Bull.

'Indeed,' said Owl, 'but, as I said, a dilemma in this case is that we don't know who the other party is that should listen to your concerns, or whether there even is another party.'

Bull took some time to mull it over. After a while he said, 'I still think it's worth a try. Will you go on strike with me?'

'Under normal circumstances I would, of course,' said Owl, 'but, unfortunately, I have some urgent business to attend to this afternoon.'

She hastily made her apologies and disappeared into the rain.

Bull concluded that, for his strike to be effective, he should first of all broaden his base, as Owl had suggested. He went from door to door to make his case, and see if he could win support.

'Will you go on strike with me to force the rain to

stop falling?' he asked Blackbird.

Blackbird was apologetic.

'I'm sorry that the rain is annoying you, Bull,' he said, 'but I can't support you with this one. In fact, I rather like the rain and hope it will continue, because it brings the earthworms up so abundantly.'

Bull also failed to get Ladybird on his side. Ladybird, always obsessed with the numbers, advised Bull that he should simply plan his life better around what was statistically unavoidable. Crocs didn't see the point of a strike and said the mud made him happy, and Goat was too preoccupied with his personal state of mind to care.

But Bull wasn't one to give up easily, and things started to move fast when he won his case with Hippo and Elephant. Together, the three took centre stage on the crossroads in the middle of the forest, their backs against each other and their front legs folded decisively. Around them they had put up banners, on which they had written powerful messages, such as *'We strike, until the rain gets on his bike!'*, and *'Big bums for justice — we demand a dry spell'*.

The trio formed a mighty obstacle and they soon attracted lots of attention. Some got annoyed by their prominent obstruction of the public road. Others just observed the protesters in amusement, shrugged their shoulders and walked on. As if a strike would help against the rain!

But when Beetle arrived, he joined the three big animals immediately because, as he explained, after a week of persistent rainfall he had practically gone deaf with the sound of the drops drumming on his back. He was as fed up as Bull, if not more.

Three hours into the strike the sound of the rain changed from a heavy drum to a much lighter tap. Then the rain stopped completely. There was only the dripping from leaves to be heard for a little while longer, and then the sun finally broke through the clouds and changed the wet forest and fields into a steaming wonder-world.

'There!' said Bull, 'that will teach them not to take us for granted next time.'

10   Showing Off

Another wonderful day was nearing its conclusion; dusk softly descending onto trees and shrubs, the river and its banks, paths and fields, and onto everyone's homes and plots — wrapping the world in a muted afterglow that was certain to touch your soul. And, as if the visual sensuality of the evening wasn't enough, Blackbird had started warming up for 'Dusk Delights', his daily programme of songs and serenades, which left practically no living heart unmoved and relieved many troubled minds from most of their worries, at least for the time being.

'Aren't we lucky to have such talent in our midst?' Owl said to Jay.

'Mmm,' Jay said. 'He's a bit of a show-off, don't you think?'

Owl was taken aback by Jay's response.

'I don't agree,' she replied. 'Blackbird is only doing what's in his nature. He's not forcing us to listen, is he? He's not making us pay for it. Where else would you find such brilliant entertainment for free?'

'I'd happily pay for him to give us a break once in a while,' Jay grumbled. 'Or, at least, make a proper show of it. He's always just sitting there in his boring black frock. Not exactly a feast for the eye. I think he's mainly doing it for his own pleasure, not caring that all of us have to put up with it. As for I, I've had enough of it.'

And he flew off into the forest, but not before making sure to unfold his flash of blue feathers close to Owl's face.

Talk about showing off, Owl huffed. If you can't

appreciate Blackbird's songs, I'd rather listen to them on my own.

But she struggled to do so. Somehow, Jay's remark had put a stain on her personal enjoyment. Why was Jay so negative about Blackbird singing?

Owl forced herself to hear the full concert, right up until the grand finale, but immediately afterwards she went to find Crocs. She soon spotted Crocs down Beech Lane, chatting to Hedgehog and Moth.

Crocs greeted Owl warmly.

'Welcome, dear friend,' he said. 'Wasn't it a brilliant show tonight? Did you hear the full recital?'

'That's what I've come to talk about, actually,' Owl said. 'Do you not think that perhaps Blackbird is making too much of it, that perhaps he's taking us all for granted?'

'Why, no,' Crocs said in surprise. 'I thought it was perfect.'

'Isn't he amazing?' Hedgehog said. 'Such talent!'

'What makes you say that?' Moth asked Owl. 'Did you not enjoy it tonight?'

'I did,' Owl said. 'Very much so. It's just that I was sitting with Jay, and he didn't like it all that much. He said Blackbird was showing off, without any regard for his audience.'

'That's rich,' Crocs said. 'What's wrong with him, to be so negative about such superb, free entertainment?'

'Jay can be funny like that,' Hedgehog observed. 'I've noticed that before.'

'He didn't shy away from showing off his feathers before he disappeared,' Owl said.

The four of them sat together, each musing over what could possibly be troubling Jay. None of them seriously thought that Blackbird could be held responsible for Jay's negativity. Then Moth had a thought. His face lit up when he spoke.

'Where we may be going wrong,' he said, 'is that we're not complimenting Jay enough on his appearance. We all know how proud he is of his special feathers, but I, for one, can't remember ever having told him how beautiful they are.'

'Neither have I,' Hedgehog and Crocs admitted simultaneously.

'Perhaps that's making him feel bitter,' Owl said. 'Perhaps he's not receiving the admiration he craves. And deserves! He always looks stunning. But the difficulty is that he's only showing us when he's already flying off.'

When it dawned on them how neglectful they had been towards Jay, how this had to be the underlying issue that must have built up over time — for much too long probably — a potential solution presented itself.

'We must organise a show,' Crocs said. 'A full-scale evening programme in which Jay will be starring. We could include some music and perhaps some other acts, but there must be no doubt that Jay will be the headline act. He must have all the time in the world to show off his feathers and be admired.'

'How about a talent show?' Hedgehog suggested. 'I've been practising some ground rolls that I'd be happy to demonstrate.'

'Poetry?' Moth asked.

'All great ideas,' Crocs said, 'as long as we make sure

that Jay can shine. No one else should steal the show.'

Crocs took it upon himself to present the concept to Jay, but not before he had consulted with Blackbird and signed him up to provide toned-down tunes for the interval slot. Cyrus and Hippo were keen to take part too, and Peacock promised to sell ice-creams without opening out his tail fan.

'You'll be the star of the show,' Crocs explained to Jay. 'We hardly ever get a chance to admire your stunning colours. Without you the show can't go ahead.'

'Could I do some stand-up, too?' Jay asked, overwhelmed by the unexpected opportunity that was presented to him.

'Even better,' Crocs smiled. 'You'll be the headline act. You must set the tone.'

Thus, the organisation of a wonderful evening of entertainment was set into motion. Billboards were put up everywhere, with 'Starring Jay' printed in the biggest letters, above a picture of Jay, in which he looked seductively over his radiant blue left wing. There was a sizeable feature in the paper and, in the run up to the big event, no conversation was had in which the excitement could be contained.

When, at long last, the show started it certainly did not disappoint. As Master of Ceremonies Crocs gave every performer their due credit and praise for sharing their talent so publicly, but he left no one in any doubt that the event had only one shining light: Jay, with his flash of blue, and the speedy sequence of his hilarious one-liners, a talent that hardly anyone had been aware of before. Jay was given all the time he needed for showing it off properly.

Many autographs were requested of Jay after the show and, in the following weeks and months, the cutting edge of his commentary was mostly taken for the wit it really was.

11 Invisible Connection

Mole and Bull were sitting together at the edge of the field, enjoying the warm day. Bull was ecstatic to feel the sunshine on his skin, but Mole was keeping in the shadow of the overhanging oak leaves, protecting her poor eyes from the bright light.

'It's so nice to have some time with you,' said Bull. 'We don't often have a chance to catch up.'

'Yes,' said Mole. 'It has been too long.'

'What's it like, down there, under my field?' asked Bull.

'Oh, it's very special,' said Mole. 'There's a whole world going on underground. The smells of the earth are just phenomenal. You must notice that yourself sometimes, when you dig away with your hoofs.'

'Indeed,' said Bull, 'the earth has a delightful aroma. I find that it varies quite a lot, too. It changes with the weather and with the time of day.'

'Exactly!' said Mole. 'Now imagine that underground those smells are ten times stronger. And there are sounds, too, coming from all directions, and tremors from deep down in the earth and from above.'

'Magic!' said Bull. 'What I absolutely love is that I can tell where you are from the heaps of earth you bring to the surface.'

'That makes two of us,' said Mole. 'Did you know that I can tell pretty precisely where you are, purely by the impact of your movements above my head?'

'Really?' asked Bull. 'Is my footstep that heavy? I didn't realise. I shall try to walk more quietly.'

'No, please don't,' said Mole. 'It gives me a lovely,

homely feeling.'

They stayed quiet for a while, simply enjoying one another's company and the magic of the invisible connection that, as they had established, existed between below and above.

After a while Bull said, 'Mole, I hope you don't mind me asking, but I always wondered how you can find your way underground, given that your eyesight is not exactly brilliant.'

'Ah,' said Mole, 'my eyesight, yes. Really, it all depends on how you look at it. You see, I know that my eyes are not as strong as yours, for example. But I know that only from hearsay. Personally, I have never known my eyes to be any different, and to me they are perfectly adequate. How do I find my way, you ask. Well, if you'll excuse the pun, there is always some light at the end of the tunnel, that gives me a general sense of direction. But the smells and sounds and tremors that I mentioned are equally important, if not more so. You could say that I see with my nose and ears, rather than with my eyes.'

'But what if you go further afield?' asked Bull. 'For example, when you go on holiday to a place where everything is different.'

'Wouldn't that be just the same as when you go away?' said Mole. 'There are always lots of different sensations, all around us. Last year, for example, I made a trip with my friend Worm. We just headed south and we saw some amazing things. Mind you, neither of us travel very fast, but not far from here we discovered this enormous underground lake. And another day's travel from there we found this incredible knot of twisted roots. It must have been one of those oak trees growing there. Worm couldn't get enough of throwing himself down the bendy slides. Do you ever go on holiday?'

'I have been on day trips,' said Bull. 'And I've read some books about other places, where it's always hot or always cold.'

'Wouldn't you like to go there?' asked Mole.

'I would,' said Bull, 'but then again I wouldn't. You see, I like it here best. Can you say that you like it best, somewhere, if you haven't been to somewhere else?'

'Don't see why not,' said Mole. 'We're just tourists in our own country. As far as I'm concerned, there's nothing wrong with that.'

Bull agreed. And so they sat together while the afternoon was slowly passing by.

'Really good to catch up,' said Bull, after a while.

'It's perfect,' said Mole. 'I'm really enjoying it.'

12   Making an Entrance

Tonight was the big night. A masked ball had been organised, taking place on the big lawn by the lake, and everyone had been invited. A band was hired to play jazz and waltzes from eight o'clock until deep into the night, and there would be champagne and nibbles, as much as you like. Imagine the excitement! It was to be a once-in-a-lifetime event. The older guests were looking forward to displaying their natural authority, to bathing in the considerable respect that their social ranks commanded. For the younger ones the long-awaited party couldn't come soon enough. It was their chance to make a debut appearance on the public stage and — hopefully — a lasting impression. Who would be the most beautiful, radiant or witty? Who would be asked to dance most and who would be most admired?

Around six in the evening a great many finishing touches were made. Hoofs and horns were polished to blinding effect, feathers and wings were brushed and realigned into their colourful patterns. Indeed, nature itself is a true artist and knows all too well how best to display its art. Only the musicians and cooks could not participate in the 'prettyfying' self-indulgence as they needed all their skill and concentration to ensure that nothing lacking in tune or taste would be served.

From seven onwards guests started to arrive. Some came early, obviously to make the most of the free drinks and snacks. Others were typically last minute. When the band finally started playing an enormous crowd had already gathered. There was Goat, with his wispy silver beard and elegantly carved horns. Frog was wearing a flowery fragrance and couldn't stop himself from saying 'How do you do?' all the time. Jay had surrounded himself with a star-struck audience, making them laugh with non-stop stories, too incredible not to be true. And Crocs, enjoying a glass of sparkling champagne, or two, oozed confidence and statesmanship with his charm and warm-hearted smiles for each and every one. But, of course, it was a masked ball, so no one knew with complete certainty who was who, although there was some pretty accurate guesswork.

One guest was notably still absent: Peacock. He was never known to be late, but this time he had a plan. He was intent on making the grandest entrance imaginable. So, he waited in the wings until the band finished their first set. Then, as the music stopped and he could be sure of everyone's full attention, he strode forward towards the gate, in all of his magnificent glory. And there he stopped.

'Look, there's Peacock' he heard, and, 'Doesn't he look fabulous!'

But the swell of pride in his throat came to a swift end when they started saying, 'Why doesn't he come and join in?'

Frog and Goat came up to him.

'You look amazing,' Goat said. 'Why don't you join us?'

Peacock didn't say a word.

'Stunning,' said Frog. 'But you're not naturally shy. Come on in. Have some champagne. Dance with me!'

'I'm stuck,' Peacock hissed, under his breath.

'What?' said Goat and Frog, who didn't immediately

understand what Peacock meant.

'I'm stuck in the gate,' said Peacock, even more embarrassed to have to spell it out.

Only now did Frog and Goat notice what stopped their friend from proceeding.

'Fold your feathers,' Goat suggested. 'Then you would easily get through the gate.'

'I can't,' said Peacock.

'Why not?' asked Frog.

'Because I have to make a grand entrance.'

'But how can you make any entrance at all if you don't even join the party?'

'Can't you take the gate down?' Peacock tried, feebly. 'Discreetly, please?'

Frog and Goat looked at each other. It seemed a reasonable request. They called Hippo and Elephant. When the issue had been explained to them, Hippo and Elephant stood nonchalantly either side of Peacock. At the count of three they knocked down the gate with a gentle kick of their hind legs. Then, they escorted Peacock — in his full regalia — to the middle of the floor, fetched him champagne, and they all danced till dawn.

Months later, in every conversation about the ball, it still came up how Peacock had outshone them all, although, strictly speaking, nobody could be certain that the glorious, masked figure had really been Peacock.

13   I Spy

Dragonfly, Crocs, Frog and Heron were hanging out at the waterside. It was one of those summer evenings, when they couldn't get enough of the sun on their skin, and when the summer and their lives seemed blissfully endless. They had little to say to each other and, really, it didn't matter. Dragonfly felt a touch awkward about it, desiring it to be more than just sitting together in silence, but she couldn't think of anything meaningful to say, so she suggested playing 'I Spy'.

Frog and Crocs weren't bothered, but Heron supported her immediately.

'A wonderful idea, Dragonfly,' he said. 'Let's play. Will you begin?'

'I spy with my little eye…' Dragonfly started, hovering over them and looking for something suitable. 'I spy something with my little eye and its colour is orange.'

'Goldfish,' said Heron, without blinking. Nothing ever escaped his gaze and although Dragonfly had tried being clever and choosing a colour that wasn't visible all the time, Heron wasn't fooled.

'How did you know?' Dragonfly asked.

'I just guessed,' said Heron.

'My turn, I have one,' said Frog. 'I spy something with my little eye of which the colour is green.'

Crocs and Dragonfly searched around. Of course, most things on the riverbank had a green hue in them, including they themselves, as well as Frog. But before they could make a first guess on what it might be, Heron said calmly: 'Lily pad'.

'Is the right answer,' said Frog, tapping on the leaf

underneath him.

'You are either very clever or very lucky,' said Dragonfly to Heron, visibly impressed.

'Just another lucky guess, I suppose,' Heron admitted. 'Give me another.'

'Try this one,' said Crocs, who had turned on his back and folded his front legs underneath his head.

'My little eye spies something of which the main colour is …'

'Sky,' Heron interrupted, before Crocs could finish his sentence.

'This is awesome,' Crocs said. 'Can you read our minds, or what?'

'It's only,' Heron explained, 'that spying is my business. I suppose I have a knack for seeing things before anybody else does.'

'Well, it's not much fun like this,' Dragonfly said. 'If it's so easy for you, you had better think of one for us to guess.'

'Can I do a riddle instead?' asked Heron. He proceeded without waiting for confirmation.

'Who am I? I have more wrinkles than can ever be told.
They grow bigger and bigger, but I never grow old.'

'Hang on,' said Crocs. 'That's complicated. Can you say that again?'

Heron repeated the riddle. Frog, Crocs and Dragonfly remained silent, trying their hardest to work out what the answer could be.

'This is too difficult,' said Dragonfly, after a while. 'Can you give us a clue?'

'The riddle is the clue,' Heron said. 'Would you like me to say it again?'

He repeated the lines of the riddle a third time.

The three stretched their brains, as far as they could go, but no answer came.

'It's just too hard,' said Dragonfly. 'Can you really not help us a little?'

'Absolutely not,' said Heron. 'If I say more, I will give it away.'

'Well, in that case I give up,' said Dragonfly, and she flew off.

'Too tricky for me, friend,' said Crocs. 'My brain hurts, I think I need a bath.'

He rolled over, into the river.

Heron looked expectantly at his last remaining friend, but Frog said: 'You are just too serious to be fun.' And he plunged off his lily pad and disappeared underwater. Heron was left on his own.

After a while a voice came from the Water.

'Nice rhyme, that,' the voice said, 'but it's not true.'

'What isn't true?' asked Heron.

'That I never get old,' said the Water.

'But you don't look old,' said Heron.

'That's just my trick,' said the Water. 'I may not look it, but I can assure you that I have been around since before the old oak tree was merely a thought.'

'Oh,' said Heron. 'I'm sorry. I didn't know that.'

'If you ask me, it's a bit late to be sorry,' said the Water. 'You'd do best to remember next time, that being clever is not all that matters.'

And with that the Water disappeared under its wrinkles.

14   Seeing your True Self

'What really frustrates me,' said Peacock to Moth, 'is that you can never really see yourself in the mirror.'

'What do you mean?' asked Moth.

'Well, if you look in the mirror,' explained Peacock, 'you don't see yourself as you really are. You can only see a mirror image of yourself, in reverse, as it were. In the mirror your right side is left and your left has become right. For example, if in the mirror your feathers on the right look a bit ruffled, they're really the feathers on your left wing. And vice versa.'

'Does that matter?' asked Moth.

'Of course, it does,' said Peacock. 'First of all, purely practically, when I go to a party, I want to feel confident that I look tip-top, and when I'm getting ready for a show I could really do without the stress of the confusion. Secondly, even more important, is that I would like to see and know myself for what I really am. The mirror only gives me a reflection, not the real thing. And because it's the wrong way round, you can never face the true you. Do you see what I mean?'

'Mm, I do,' said Moth. 'This is pretty deep stuff. Let me think about it for a little while.'

And he went home to give the whole issue some private thought.

The next morning Moth came hurrying back, carrying his own mirror under his wing. He knocked on Peacock's door and called out.

'I have a solution, Peacock.'

Peacock let him in, surprised to see the excitement

on Moth's face.

'Look,' said Moth. 'Yesterday you explained to me, that what you see in the mirror is not the real you, but the wrong-way-round-you, so to speak. So I thought; all we need to do, is have two mirrors in front of each other, so that we can turn the wrong-way-round-you back into the right-way-round-you, the real you.

'That's a brilliant idea,' said Peacock. 'Let's try it.'

They put both their mirrors opposite each other, and Peacock stepped in between them. But, just like before, he could only see his mirrored self.

'It doesn't work,' he said. 'When I step in between the mirrors, I can only see myself in the mirror in front of me, but not in the other one, because I'm blocking my view.'

'Mmm,' said Moth, disappointed that his solution didn't work.

'What about if we put the mirrors on a slight angle, and you try looking fractionally past yourself?'

They experimented with various positions, leaning mirrors against chairs and on stacks of books, trying to find the right angle. Finally, they seemed to have found the right set up, but Peacock became confused.

'In this way I can't see all of me,' he said, 'but the bit of me that I can see, I now see ten, no a hundred, no maybe a thousand times. How do I know which one of those is the real me?'

Moth tried it, too, and saw what Peacock meant. In the two mirrors — placed cleverly opposite each other, but at a slight angle — the reflection of himself was repeated many times. He looked like a dazzling cloud of wings. It wasn't working.

That evening Moth paid Peacock another visit. Peacock looked gloomy and had his back turned to the mirror.

'I'm sorry that the trick with the mirrors didn't resolve the issue,' Moth said. 'As a consolation, I have written a poem for you. I often find that poems are very good to discover the true nature of things.'

He handed Peacock a piece of paper, on which was written:

To my dear friend Peacock

If in doubt, come running
and I will tell you you look stunning

'That doesn't make sense,' said Peacock. 'I don't understand what it says.'

'I know,' said Moth, suppressing a wicked smile. 'But as I said, poems can be very helpful, even though they don't appear to make sense instantly. It's a bit like your mirror. You look at it, but it's often not immediately clear who or what you actually see. Why don't you stick it on the wall? Maybe, after a while, it will start making more sense.'

Without waiting for Peacock's approval he pinned his poem onto the wall and left his friend to it.

Peacock was rather bewildered by the poetic gift but thought it would be rude to remove the paper with the strange words, so he left it on his wall. Later that evening, when he was getting ready for a dinner party, he caught a glimpse in his mirror of the paper on the opposite wall. (Moth, of course, had placed it there on purpose!)

Instantly his friend's words fell into place.

'Ha!' Peacock laughed out loud. 'I should stop making things so complicated for myself.'

15 Between a Rock and a Hard Place

'What's the point?' asked Worm. 'Everything is going to pot and whatever I do, the result will be the same. It makes absolutely no difference.'

Mole observed her friend in surprise.

'I've never known you to be so downbeat,' she said.

'I'm sorry, Mole,' said Worm. 'I don't mean to drag you along in my bout of despair. It's just that everything seems to be against me today, which is utterly upsetting.'

'Tell me more,' Mole said. 'I have time.'

'Are you sure?' Worm asked. 'I don't want to bore you with the whole story.'

'You've made me curious,' Mole said. 'It's a while since I was told a story. As long as you have a good plot?'

'That's exactly the issue,' Worm said. 'I don't want to be dramatic about it, but I've started wondering if this plot is all wrong, if I have been wasting a lot of my time here, whilst it could have been so much better elsewhere.'

It took Mole a few seconds to realise that Worm wasn't talking about the plot to his story, but about the actual plot of land where they were now sitting and conversing.

'What's wrong with this one, then?' she asked. 'I've never found any fault with it.'

'Neither have I,' said Worm, 'until this morning. I have spent many happy years here, but when I woke up today, everything was topsy-turvy. Nothing is where it should be, all the things I was working on yesterday seem to have vanished, whichever way I turn there suddenly appears to be a mountain of stones to climb over and — worst of all — I can't find my earplugs anywhere.'

It wasn't quite the story Mole had hoped for. Worm's outburst seemed chaotic, as if her friend had lost himself, rather than his earplugs, but as she had already promised Worm her listening time, she felt duty-bound to hear him out.

'What do you need those for?' she asked.

'My earplugs? Oh, I use them early mornings, when Blackbird is hopping about above my head. Wearing earplugs saves me the effort of getting up and telling him to go somewhere else. I'm not always in the mood for a chat first thing.'

'I see,' Mole said. 'And you couldn't find them this morning? Could you have just mislaid them? Anyway, you'd better start at the beginning, to give me the full picture. Talk me through your day, as it were.'

It was a very generous invitation. Everybody knew that Worm was a stickler for detail and that, given the time, he talked rather slowly, sometimes repeating parts of his narrative. But Mole knew that aired frustrations more easily float away into the blue sky and that, if she succeeded in bringing her friend's heart rate back down, they could both look forward to an enjoyable evening. And even though, now and again, she felt herself almost slipping away into a drowsy slumber, she managed to keep Worm's story going with cleverly injected requests for clarification or reflection, such as: 'So you were heading towards the nettles?' or; 'Could the heavy rain have caused that?'

'You can see, can't you?' Worm said, having finally

reached the conclusion of his drawn-out report, 'that I find myself caught between a rock and a hard place? Should I chuck it all in, and move somewhere else altogether, or should I pretend nothing like this actually happened, and start from scratch again tomorrow morning?'

Mole sat up straight to emphasize she had, really, been deeply involved in Worm's narrative.

'Definitely, I can see that,' she agreed. 'Between a rock and a hard place, that's a good way of putting it. It's a dilemma, isn't it? I'd miss you terribly, though, if you were to move away, and so would others, I'm sure. Blackbird, for one. He would miss you, with or without your earplugs. They must be somewhere, don't you think? And if they don't turn up, couldn't you get yourself a new set?'

'I guess so,' Worm said. 'Well, that settles it, then. I'll just stay, I think. Fingers crossed tomorrow will bring a better day.'

He thanked Mole for her patient listening and kind words.

'Don't mention it,' Mole said. 'I'm convinced it's the right decision and, for me, well, it's just a relief to know that you're staying. Drinks? I feel we've deserved it. The moon should be coming up soon.'

16 Time Off

It was a long time since Bumblebee had taken a day off. She wasn't sure that she should take time off, because she liked what she did. She enjoyed being outside, preferably in the sunshine, but she didn't mind the occasional spot of rain. It made everything smell so good. She liked to be among the flowers and felt more satisfied when she was active. So why take time off?

It was Crocs who had suggested she should.

'Take some time off,' Crocs had advised. 'You're always so busy.'

'I like being busy,' Bumblebee had answered. 'What is wrong with being busy?'

'There's nothing wrong with being busy,' Crocs had said, 'except that being busy doesn't leave you much time to see the rest of the world.'

Bumblebee couldn't stop thinking about what Crocs had said. Was she missing out on something? Should she take a break, even though she didn't feel she needed one? These questions cast a shadow over her otherwise enjoyable tasks. At night the thought kept her awake that she might have lived and played too close to home, as it were, that she had foolishly believed that her own small world was as big as the universe.

The next morning, she made up her mind.

'Live now or not at all,' she said to herself, as she was getting a few things together for the travel plans she was setting into motion. When she had finished packing, she flew to Bull to let someone know she would be away for a while.

'A holiday, how wonderful!' said Bull. 'Where are

you going?'

'Not a holiday. Travelling,' said Bumblebee, not liking the idea of being a tourist. 'I'm going south. No particular place. Just checking it out, you know.'

'Have a good time travelling,' Bull said wholeheartedly. 'Please send us a postcard, if you have the chance.'

Bumblebee set off towards the South. She wasn't quite sure how far south she would go, and she didn't want to be sure. The vagueness of it excited her, and it made her a little nervous, too, which was exciting in itself.

As she went further and further south, she saw many different things. Not things that were incomprehensibly different, nothing she hadn't seen before or at least heard about, but things similar to the things she knew, albeit in different shapes and colours. Flowers were a deeper kind of yellow in the South. The earth was more red. Hills were higher, lakes were bluer.

'This is so incredible,' she said to herself, many times. 'Aren't I the lucky one, just flying around here with nothing to do other than take in all this wonder?'

She would ponder over the right words for describing everything she saw to her friends at home, over the best way to express all of his newly gained experience of being free and foreign.

But after a week her mood started to dull. She wondered about this and felt guilty, too, realising she no longer enjoyed travelling as much as she felt she ought to.

'I'm just full up,' she concluded. 'I've seen so many new things. I can't take any more in.'

She thought that, probably, it was time to make her way home.

Flying back, she saw many more new and beautiful things and she didn't stop admiring them. She knew that, for a traveller, every day must be special and that even the road back home was still a new adventure. But the closer she came to home, the louder her heart started beating and, when she finally arrived back in familiar territory, a particular kind of peace came over her.

Crocs and Bull were quick to drop by when they heard that Bumblebee was back.

'How was it?' they wanted to know. 'Did you see amazing things?'

'Amazing!' said Bumblebee. 'It was absolutely wonderful. I saw so many things; my eyes could hardly take it all in. The flowers are a different yellow down south, and the hills are much higher. How have things been around here?'

'Oh, pretty good,' said Bull. 'Same as ever. It must be so nice to take a break.'

'Absolutely, I thoroughly recommend it,' said Bumblebee. 'It gives you a different outlook on things. I don't know why I never before thought of taking time off.'

17   Meeting of the Minds

It was one of those lazy afternoons on the riverbank, when normally everything and everybody would be still and quiet; no clouds in the sky, not a breath of wind and only the sun sending its soothing rays down to warm the earth and its inhabitants. It was the kind of afternoon when everybody would just be and wait — not causing a stir or longing for action; just breathing.

Not today, though. A crowd had gathered, all suitably sorted with refreshments and sun umbrellas. In the middle of the riverbank a small table with two chairs had been set up. Just arriving centre stage to take their seats were Crocs and Frog, both finalists in 'Meeting of the Minds'.

Meeting of the Minds was one of the biggest events of the year. It was a quiz show, but without any exact questions or answers, because, as the inventors of the series had stated,

'To so many questions in life there is no single, unambiguous answer, no absolute right or wrong. Therefore, the best we can and should do is discuss the complicated world around us and try to achieve a level of understanding of it.'

Contestants in the competition were asked to offer one another topics that would enable deep and meaningful thought. In reality, 'contestants' was not the most accurate description of the candidates. Participants would perhaps be a better word, because Meeting of the Minds didn't have a winner, as such. The outcome would merely be an informal assessment from the audience about what thought had, by popular consensus, been most appreciated. This year Crocs and Frog had both made it through to the final, that was now about to begin.

'My dear, honourable friend, Frog,' started Crocs. 'It is such a delight to be conversing with you today. May I have your thoughts on the qualities of air?'

A rumble went through the audience. This question was full on and straight in, indeed. But Frog wasn't fazed by it.

'Thank you, Crocs, for sharing the stage with me, and giving me this wonderful subject to start off on,' he said. 'Air is a subject close to my heart. It is, like love, one of the most precious things we have. And have not, I should add. We can capture air, for a moment or so, in our lungs or in a bubble rising quickly through the water in the river, but then we must let go. And we must trust that there will always be new air to take in, even though we can't see air, as air is — again, like love — invisible. The defining quality of air is that it's as much in us as we are in it. I believe that air is part of our soul.'

A whisper of admiration rolled through the audience, while Frog prepared his counter challenge.

'Most respected Crocs,' he said. 'Will you share with me, and with our distinguished audience, your understanding of time?'

'With the greatest pleasure,' Crocs replied, without delay. 'We all know that time travels at a regular pace, since every day's journey from dawn to dusk is part of the solar clockwork that regulates our universe. Time is so much bigger than we are. We seem to have no hold on it. But I ask, is its overwhelming and unstoppable pace really the true nature of time? Do we not find that a second may last for hours, whilst an hour may pass in the blink of an eye? I believe that time is not a passing trade, not something that slips through our fingers to then be lost forever. My theory is more comforting. I believe that time is, rather like a book, a story that begins and grows, yet which, as it develops, also remains what it was on the first page. Take me, for example. Here I am, Crocs, middle-aged and well-respected, I hope. Time has travelled through my cells and my bones, but I'm also still the little baby Crocs that I was when my story began. That little Crocs is still inside me, together with all his older alter egos. I think time can be your friend, if you let it be, but, if you try to put time in a box, you'll soon find that box empty.'

Crocs' words caused a smile on many faces. He always had that personal touch. He knew how to bring an abstract theme close to home. Now it was his turn again to suggest a topic.

'Comrade Frog, will you explain for us your perception of freedom?'

'Freedom is an interesting thing,' said Frog. 'We are all born free and yet we are all caught in a body, a skin, in our heads, our souls, and in a moment of time and history. Most important is perhaps that we are caught up in a world of consequences. I'm free to go or stay, for example, even at this very moment — although I wouldn't want to disappoint our audience. I'm free to sit on a leaf or dive into the water, but there's more to it. Whatever I choose to do effects everything and everyone that isn't me. For example, someone else could choose to sit on my leaf once I have vacated it, but they can't swim where I have jumped in. And it goes on. As I see it, freedom is a gift to us, not one that we own, but one we must earn. And you, admirable master of charms, will you delight me and our audience on the subject of love?'

'You touch my heart with that invitation, Frog,' Crocs replied. 'You yourself have already spoken about love so eloquently. Wholeheartedly do I agree with you that love is a mystery we can't do without. I would like to focus on the strange duality of love. Take being in love, for example. Is this an act of giving, of honouring with gifts someone other than ourselves, going out of our way to please and make happy? Or is it firstly an act of wanting, desiring, willing the other to be there for us? Anyone who has had the true experience of love will agree that it must be both; an equilibrium of being both selfish and selfless — although that last word is not well chosen, because to be able to love, to give and take, I'm convinced that there must be a self. And then, there are often conflicting feelings of love. For example, I dearly love you as my friend, but at the same time I would also dearly love to be the winner of tonight's event, even though that might break your heart. From that point of view, it is — on second thought — a relief that you are so clever and well-spoken, leaving me little chance of causing you that pain.'

In this manner of discourse, the evening went on into the small hours. The Stars twinkled in the dark night sky. The audience felt mellowed by so many stunning observations from both finalists about the nature of the world and how beautiful life on earth was. It was hardly possible to decide who should be crowned the winner. In the end the difficult task of 'declaring' was left to Owl.

'The way I see it,' Owl said, 'and as already understood by those who initiated this wonderful event, is that to many questions in life there is no clear answer. The question of who has, this evening, spoken most eloquently, Frog or Crocs, and who has enlightened us most is — fortunately, I hasten to add — one of those unanswerable questions. Therefore, I declare that this year's Meeting of the Minds must remain inconclusive. We should all go to bed and sleep safely in the knowledge that we have such reassuring resources of wisdom among us.

And so they did. Crocs and Frog heartily embraced and congratulated each other. And many more hours after everyone had left, they could still be found at the riverside, discussing the marvels of the universe.

18   No Half Measures

Beetle and Bumblebee, who lived next door to each other, were both busy dragging large planks of wood from the forest and nailing them to their porches, leaving only the tiniest gap to allow them to enter and exit their houses. When everything was pretty much sealed off, bar the small opening, they proceeded to tie everything up with strong rope, which they then secured at ground level with heavy stones. Bull, who happened to walk by, observed their work with a mixture of wonder and admiration.

'I see you two are taking no half measures,' he said. 'May I inquire after the reason for your elaborate constructions? They look ingenious, although perhaps also a touch unsightly.'

'Belt and braces, mate,' Beetle said. 'You may laugh, but now is not the time to risk life and limb.'

'Perhaps you haven't heard,' Bumblebee added. She was clearly exhausted and wiped the sweat from her brow. 'There's a storm brewing. A big one. Ladybird could tell from her charts.'

'No, I have not heard that,' Bull said. He looked up at the blue sky, where the big yellow sun was relentlessly firing on all cylinders, and where not a sliver of cloud or a whisper of wind was noticeable.

'Doesn't feel as if bad weather is on its way,' he said. 'When did Ladybird say we should expect it?'

'Can't remember the particulars,' Bumblebee said. 'Ladybird just told us that it's on its way and that it will be bad.'

'You precious creatures do well to prepare for the

worst,' said Bull. 'You don't want to be overcome by any such freak event.'

He smiled, not quite believing that it could be as bad as they thought.

'Indeed not,' said Beetle. He had just tightened the last rope and started squeezing himself through the gap. 'Better to be safe than sorry.'

Bull continued his stroll in the sunshine. When he came to the river, he immediately noticed there was a surge of activity there, too. Crocs had folded up his deckchairs and was pulling a tarpaulin over the stacks they formed on his veranda. Frog was busy turning over his flotilla of lily pads and tying them down.

'So that they won't get ripped to pieces,' he said.

And Heron was creating a sturdy-looking flood defence from rocks and reeds.

'To avoid anything above knee-deep, which I hate,' he explained, without stopping.

Only Fish had time to talk.

'They're expecting all kinds of weather,' she said. 'Apparently, it's the latest prediction from Ladybird, who is never wrong. Nobody wants to be caught out. Half measures won't do.'

'Aren't you concerned about it, then?' Bull asked.

Fish shook her head.

'Naah,' she said. Shouldn't affect me much. I'll just have to stay put when it hits.'

Again, Bull looked up at the sky. There was still no sign of change up there. Not at all. He decided to find Ladybird and ask for more specific details on the looming upheaval. Always best to hear it from the horse's mouth, metaphorically speaking.

On his way to Ladybird, he saw Owl taking boxes of books from her library in the oak tree to a solid chest with heavy metal bands in a corner of the old barn. He stopped to look at Owl's execution of the delicate task.

'The most precious thing I have,' Owl explained. 'The oak is fine as protection against wind and rain, but if lightening were to strike, that would be the end of the story. Everything would go up in flames. Can't risk it.'

Owl's words and actions made Bull more nervous. There was still no cloud in the sky, but it was a seriously hot day. Owl could be right, he thought. There might well be thunder and lightning ere the day was done.

But, unlike all the others, Ladybird seemed not in the least concerned about the bad weather she had predicted. Bull found her outside on her veranda, deeply engrossed in a magazine, with a drink by her side. She was totally relaxed.

'Ladybird, is it true that a storm is heading our way? Everyone is very concerned about it and making preparations.'

'Absolutely,' Ladybird confirmed. 'Didn't you see the note I pinned up about it? At a quarter past six this evening, if I'm not mistaken.'

'At that exact time? How can you predict it so precisely?'

'Well, give or take a minute or two,' Ladybird said. 'As for your second question, that's hard to explain in a few words. Let's call it the dark science of meteorology and statistics.'

'Then, why aren't you taking precautions yourself? Why aren't you battening down your hatches?'

'Oh, I'm fully prepared,' Ladybird said. 'I don't believe in leaving things to the last minute, or to chance, for that matter. With the click of a button I can be totally secure.'

She demonstrated what she meant and pressed a button at the base of her chair. Somewhere a spring was released and, with one big swoop, Ladybird's veranda, including her chair, drink, magazine and the owner herself were — like a drawbridge — pulled upwards and inwards towards the security of Ladybird's home, which instantly looked more like an unscalable fortress than a luxury villa. It took a little more effort to get the whole contraption down again and, unfortunately, Ladybird's drink had splashed all over her, but Bull was seriously impressed. He was getting more nervous, too! He rushed home to his field and started securing as much as he could in the few hours he had left before the storm was due to arrive.

At a quarter past six exactly the first lightning strike pierced the skies, soon to be followed by a thunderclap, and more lightning and rumbles. This overture unleashed a torrent of wind and rain seldom seen before. The sky demons slashed through the forest, raged over the river and hammered on lawns and fields. Trees were groaning, with their branches violently swinging back and forth. Paths and streams did their utmost to guide nature's wrath of wind and water to safer ground.

In their dwellings everyone sat quietly, listening to the fury outside. No one suffered too much anxiety or distress, because nobody had taken half measures only. Even Bull got through the assault unscathed. How blessed they all felt, having in their midst someone like Ladybird, who had forewarned them of the turbulent weather and of the time it would strike.

19   Shooting Star

'If only,' Goat said, more to himself than to anyone in particular, 'if only I wasn't always such a wimp.'

Fish, who happened to be swimming in the vicinity, overheard him.

'Excuse me, Goat,' Fish said. 'I don't mean to intrude, but I accidentally heard you talking — to yourself I presume — and I must strongly disagree with you. I have never found you to be in the least wimpish.'

Goat was slightly annoyed that his private words had been overheard by Fish, but he was also pleased that Fish had found reason to dispute him.

'That's kind of you, Fish,' he said, 'but perhaps you don't have the full picture. You have probably never seen the other side of me. In fact, it's most likely that you haven't seen it, as I don't tend to put it on display.'

'Precisely my point,' said Fish. 'Apologies for being pedantic, but firstly — if I overheard you correctly — you were talking about always being a wimp, while you, just now, admitted that you only occasionally show that side of yourself and, therefore, not all of the time. Secondly and essentially; even from knowing you only by your good side, as you say, I can assure you that you bear none of the characteristics. None at all! Trust me, friend, there is not an ounce of wimpishness about you.'

'Really?' Goat asked. Fish had spoken so passionately and with such conviction, that it was hard not to believe her. But then Goat remembered again how long it had taken him to finally talk to Owl and Moth about his deeper feelings, and how long it had taken him after that to decide how to handle his inner turmoil. And what had he, at long last, decided to do? Absolutely nothing! He had thought it best not to take any risks, not to face his troubles head on, but just hope that they would pass. If that kind of behaviour wasn't that of a wimp, then what was?

He considered whether he should try to explain all of this to Fish; whether his friend would be understanding and sympathise, or instead ridicule him. After all, how could someone as carefree as Fish ever understand the complicated workings of his heart and soul? But way before Goat made up his mind, Fish was already continuing her attempt of reassurance.

'Absolutely!' Fish said. 'One hundred percent positive! If I'm not mistaken, you're probably still thinking about the episode of love sickness that you suffered. I must confess that Crocs told me about it. Rest assured, it was in a private chat we had, but I could tell how much that had affected you. He was concerned about you, you see, having found you so lost and at the mercy of these incomprehensible passions. Would I be right in thinking you consider your helplessness in having such feelings of dark distress evidence of you being a wimp? If that is the case, I must so very strongly disagree with you. Ha, being in love. What can be more courageous? It's a place where only the very brave amongst us dare to go. I wish I had the guts.'

'Really?' Goat asked again.

'Sure as hell,' Fish said. 'Have you heard anyone else talk about being in love? Personally, I mean? Perhaps Bumblebee has come closest, but she is so seriously romantic and so easily moved, that it's hard to tell how deep it really goes with her. No, as far as I'm aware, no one has taken it as far as you have, whether that was with your good side or the other side. If I were granted one wish to come true, it would be that I was brave enough to follow in your footsteps in this respect.'

By now, very much cheered by the ongoing praise coming from Fish, Goat had started positively glowing. He already stood up straighter and he was holding his head a lot higher again, so that his handsome horns were sparkling in the sunlight.

'Well, thank you, Fish,' he said. 'It's doing me a world of good, talking to you. Perhaps I must reconsider things. You have been so kind to me. I owe you a debt of gratitude.'

'Not at all,' said Fish. 'If anything, it's the other way round. And please accept my apologies again. I didn't mean to eavesdrop on you talking to yourself.'

Fish disappeared and left Goat in an ecstatic state of mind, super-charged and re-energised. In fact, Goat decided to go for a walk and perhaps pay Crocs a visit, talk about the good old days — if Crocs was around.

Fish, however, had been left restless by the conversation with her friend. Late at night she still found herself jumping in and out of the water. Just as she was doing so, her eye caught a shooting star, high in the sky above.

'A stroke of luck,' she said to herself. 'What shall I wish for?'

20   What's the Plan?

'So?'

Peacock looked impatient. Hippo responded somewhat sheepishly.

'So…? What do you mean?'

'So, what's the plan?' Peacock clarified. 'We've come here to help, so what would you like us to do?'

'Of course,' Hippo now said. 'What to do? It's brilliant of you to help. I don't know how I would manage without you. Ah, but Crocs isn't here yet. Perhaps we could give it a few more minutes before we start?'

Peacock was about to comment again, but Owl spoke first, applying her voice of authority.

'That seems sensible,' she said. 'If you explain what needs to happen to all of us at once, then we will all be able to act as one, and sing from the same song-sheet.'

Hippo was very grateful for Owl's interjection. Owl, at least, understood that she needed a little time to get her thoughts in order.

If the truth be known, she could have managed the house move on her own but last night, when she told her friends about her plan to settle a little way further down the river, all of them had so immediately and spontaneously said they would assist with the operation, that it had felt impossible to object.

'Congratulations,' Elephant had said, slapping her jovially on her shoulders.

'Wise move,' Owl had added.

Only Peacock had been more reserved, wanting to know whether moving only a few hundred yards down river was worth the trouble. But, as Bull, Crocs and Bumblebee had also applauded her enthusiastically, Peacock soon decided not to be the odd one out and had signed up to help with the rest of them. Before Hippo realised how fast things were unfolding, they had agreed to meet at her current address at eight o'clock this morning, which was now. That Crocs was less punctual could have been expected and was, to be honest, a relief. At least, it bought her some time.

Yes, if the truth be known, Hippo preferred to do things by herself and take everything a little more slowly. Oh yes, she understood that it was enormously generous of Bull, Crocs, Elephant, Owl, Bumblebee and Peacock to grant her a portion of their time, as they all had lives to live, too, and she was fully aware that Peacock didn't like twiddling his thumbs, and that Bumblebee hated idling. But she hadn't forced them to offer help, had she? She hadn't insisted that they all show up at this ungodly hour, when she was still half asleep and in no way able to start dishing out instructions. As if she would be ready to do that at any time at all! She never minded doing as she was told, but she was quite averse to organising others. Yet, she couldn't be ungrateful, could she?

'Apologies for being a touch late,' Crocs said. 'Didn't mean to make you all wait. So, where do we start? It's next door to Heron, isn't it, your new place?'

'Yep, that's the one,' Hippo said. 'Heron and I have always been good friends, and the southerly aspect down there is much better than what I have here.'

But Peacock's patience for small talk had run out. With his critical gaze he had already inspected all corners of Hippo's dwelling during the last few minutes.

'So, we're taking everything in here? Have you organised packing boxes?'

'There's more stuff in the back,' Hippo said, feebly, 'and some more in the garden, too.'

Peacock, Bull, Crocs, Elephant, Bumblebee and Owl now all looked around them and then back at Hippo, all eager to start. Hippo had to accept that her options for enabling further delay were used up, and that it was time to talk straight.

'Listen,' she started, 'forgive me, but I must confess that I haven't thought things through very well. Not at all, to be honest. I'm not very good at making plans. You probably knew that, anyway, didn't you? If you'd rather not help and prefer to go home... I don't want to waste your precious time.'

Owl stroked her chin, Peacock huffed, Bumblebee had already half turned around, but Crocs, who still stood in the doorway, smiled and said:

'No worries, Hippo, that's no problem at all. Plan or no plan, what could be more precious for us than helping a friend? We'll sort it out. Why don't you go over to the new place, ahead of us, and take care of refreshments? Before you can count to ten, we'll be over there with all your belongings. Leave it to us.'

'Really?' Hippo asked.

'Absolutely,' Peacock said. As soon as he realised there was a genuine chance to take control and organise the others, the look of impatience had melted from his face. 'We'll take care of it.'

And that's how it happened. No sooner had Hippo

poured out the drinks at her new place, her friends appeared, carrying — as instructed by Peacock — all her things in orderly fashion. Everything was carefully packed and labelled. They put everything in a corner of Hippo's new home, wiped the sweat from their brows, and took the refreshments that Hippo offered them.

'Honestly, I don't know how I would have managed without your help,' Hippo said. 'When I have everything back in the right place, you must all come back, so that I can thank you properly.'

'Don't mention it,' Bumblebee replied. 'Many hands make light work.'

It wasn't even lunch time yet when they had all disappeared and left Hippo to make a start with getting her new home in order. She looked at her belongings in the corner of the new home.

Most of that can wait, she thought. I wonder if Heron is about. I ought to let him know I've arrived.

21   The Bigger Picture

'Do you ever wonder why we are here?' Elephant asked.

'Not really,' Cyrus said. 'I guess we have to be somewhere. We're not in the ocean or on top of the mountains. We're not in the desert or in the rainforest. We're just here. That's ok with me, although I wouldn't mind venturing over there some time, on a sunny day.'

'Where?' Elephant asked.

'Over there,' Cyrus said.

He pointed southwards, beyond the edge of the forest.

'I've heard there's less rain that way, or, at least, less often, and that they play different kinds of music down south.'

'I've heard that, too,' Elephant said. 'Perhaps we could go together, some time. But that's not what I meant. What I meant was: Why are we here at all? Why do we exist?'

'Mmm,' Cyrus said. 'I may need more time to think about that.'

'What I mean is,' Elephant continued, getting into his stride, 'what is the reason behind us? As it stands, we all just go about our daily business without worrying too much. Sometimes it's sunny, other times there's rain. Sometimes we're busy, but on other days we do nothing at all. One moment we may be lucky, and everything is going well, and the next, whatever we try brings failure. Why? What's it all for? Do you have any idea?'

'Mmm,' Cyrus said, again. 'That's quite a complicated scenario you're sketching. If you put it like that, I start to feel rather confused. Are you telling me you're not happy, that you'd rather not be here?'

'Not at all,' Elephant said, hastily. 'No, that's not what I'm trying to say. I was simply wondering about things. You see, there are moments when I feel really good, when I'm pleased with what I'm doing and when I'm convinced that it really matters. In fact, I feel like that most of the time. But sometimes, when I'm in the middle of doing something, I suddenly start doubting myself. I start thinking that, maybe, my being here is a bit of a fluke, that I'm a mere coincidence, and that perhaps there is no reason at all behind me, behind us all.'

Cyrus tried to control his tendency to turn his head round, every time Elephant said, 'behind us'. He realised this was not the right time for being funny.

'Mmm,' he said instead, for the third time.

'Forgive me, I may sound pragmatic, Elephant, but are you perhaps making a mountain out of one of Mole's hills? Introspection is a good thing, but you can have too much of it. Would it not be better to keep your considerations more down to earth and first consider your personal identity; think about who you are and what you like, or who you would like to be, before tackling those abstract and universal questions that you seem to want an answer to?'

'Universal, indeed,' Elephant said, 'but that's exactly what I'm getting at. I'm only asking: what's the point of trying to work out who you are, if the bigger picture might not add up, if the whole universe is perhaps merely an accident? In that scenario, wouldn't it be a waste of time to limit oneself to navel-gazing?'

Cyrus began to lose his patience.

'That would be starting at the wrong end,' he said. He didn't fully succeed in keeping his voice neutral. He swallowed and started again.

'Simple question, Elephant: Do you like me? Do you like talking to me, here and now?'

Of course, Elephant did. He was about to answer Cyrus in the affirmative, but right at that moment Bumblebee came buzzing by.

'Morning, chaps,' Bumblebee said. 'Wonderful day! Can't stop. I have things to do.'

No sooner had she bumbled on than Crocs appeared along the river path, jogging with his headphones on and constantly checking some sort of time keeping or distance measuring device. He appeared not to even notice them, nor Bull, who approached from the other side, and who was busy brushing dirt off his chest.

'How do I look?' Bull asked. 'I'm meeting Mole for a picnic. Sorry, didn't mean to interrupt. Mustn't be late.'

Clearly, Bull was not seriously concerned about his looks. At least, he didn't bother waiting for an answer. As he marched onwards, Eagle catapulted down from the sky and landed on one of Elephant's tusks.

'Are you two not going to hear Heron's talk?' she asked. 'He's doing something on different ways of seeing, something about colour and movement, with time for questions at the end.'

'Do you fancy it?' Cyrus asked Elephant, relieved to have an opportunity for changing the subject of their conversation.

'Why not?' Elephant said. 'Let's do it. Do you want a lift?'

As the three of them headed towards the central square in the forest, where such events normally took place, Elephant said:

'Cyrus, on the other question..., of course, I do! More than anything.'

Fortunately, Eagle didn't ask what they had been talking about. It would have taken rather a lot of explaining.

22 The Search

'Have you seen Fish this morning?' Bumblebee asked Frog.

'I'm afraid not,' Frog said. 'As a matter of fact, I haven't seen her for a while. Is anything up?'

'Probably not,' Bumblebee said. 'I was just wondering. Normally she's making a song and dance during the early hours, but, as far as I'm aware, it's been quiet over the river recently. Just hope she's ok.'

Bumblebee's concern, initially small, soon started to grow and became infectious. Frog asked Crocs, Crocs asked Goat, Goat asked Moth, Moth asked Heron. None of them had seen or heard anything from Fish since at least last Friday. Their faces became more serious, their pacing more considered. Hippo hadn't seen a sign of Fish either, nor had Eagle, who could be relied on to pinpoint anyone or anything deep down below her, if she had a clear line of vision. And as the news — or rather, the lack of news — went round, everyone was, somehow, drawn to the waterside where hopefully — very hopefully — they wouldn't witness the unfolding of a tragedy.

'We must search the river,' Peacock suggested. 'We have no time to lose. I sincerely hope she hasn't drowned.'

'That doesn't seem likely,' Owl said. 'As long as she's in water, she should be alright. Searching the banks would be more logical, if you ask me.'

But Peacock didn't agree with Owl's logic.

'Unless she got stuck somewhere,' he said. 'If she accidentally swam into a tight spot and she can't turn around, she could drown from hunger.'

Owl had to admit that there was a faint possibility that this could have happened, even though Fish had a reputation for being one of the most agile among them. But if their friend was in trouble, be it on land or in water, they should leave no stone unturned, and they must find her alive, and soon! Every minute could be important.

They split themselves up into four search parties, each with their own captain, to ensure that every square inch of the earthly paradise that was home to them all would be combed through with the utmost precision and diligence. Peacock agreed to leave the river search to Crocs, Frog, Hippo and Heron — as long as it was done properly — whilst he himself led a group on the near riverbank. The far riverbank was checked inch by inch by Bull, Mole and Squirrel, while Eagle, Moth, Jay, Ladybird and Owl formed a squadron, crossing the sky in tight formation, again and again, scanning the valley for any sighting of Fish beneath their wings.

The search went on all afternoon — alas, without success. It was hard to tell what weighed heavier on all their hearts and minds: desperation, exhaustion or the throat-tightening fear of having lost Fish. But in the end, as the gloomy dusk turned to a breathless black, they had to give up and call off their rescue mission. There was no sign of Fish, none at all. Fish was gone.

Owl called everyone together.

'We have done everything we can,' she said, gravely. 'We have looked everywhere, and we can't possibly continue any longer, not without risking even greater loss. All we can do now is go home and hope for a miracle.'

With heavy hearts they dispersed to their separate homes, hoping that somehow Fish might have escaped a terrible fate, but despairing that she might not have. Hardly anyone got a wink of sleep that night. All were thinking of Fish.

The next morning, Bumblebee was up earlier than ever. I must get back to the river, she thought. If there is still a chance, it will be there.

She found the river shrouded in wafer-thin white mist, more beautiful than she had ever seen it. Frog was already there, staring sadly over the water.

'Any news?' Bumblebee asked, though from the expression on Frog's face she already knew the answer.

'Nope,' Frog croaked, biting his bottom lip.

They sat together, staring, not speaking, watching the white mist slowly rise towards heaven and dissolve.

All of a sudden, Fish leapt from the water, starting her daily morning dancing. At first, she didn't see Frog and Bumblebee, but when she noticed them, she called out to them:

'You two are up early! Isn't the river beautiful at this time of day? You're sitting there so harmoniously. Might there be romance brewing between the two of you? Or is that a cheeky question?'

Frog and Bumblebee ignored the suggestion.

'Where have you been?' they called out in unison. 'We haven't seen you for days.'

'I was on a retreat,' Fish said. 'Five days, other side of the falls. No speaking allowed, only meditation. I felt I needed to cleanse my soul. Has done me a world of good, but it's nice to be back home again. Why?'

Frog and Bumblebee looked at each other. The falls! Why had nobody thought to check there?

'No matter,' Frog said. 'Just ignore us.'

'Lovely moves,' Bumblebee added. 'Keep going, we like seeing you dance.'

23   Echoes from the Past

Crocs and Frog could be seen walking side by side at a leisurely pace on the path along the river. It was a route favoured by many; first a good stretch alongside the water, then a right turn into Beech Lane, up to the crossroads with Hazel Avenue, which led straight to the central square in the forest, featuring comfortable seats in dappled sunlight. After a short rest you could then return to the river via the Bramble Track shortcut or go somewhere else altogether.

On Thursday mornings, however, which was the regular strolling time for Frog and Crocs, others mostly stayed clear and made sure, if they could help it, not to get in the way of the learned exchanges between the respected couple. Both characters usually walked in the calmest of manners, only occasionally making an expressive gesture to illuminate a point they were making.

'This is something the ancient thinkers understood so well,' Crocs said. 'Walking and talking, the invigorating qualities that fresh air in a natural environment brings to thought and conversation.'

He looked briefly over his shoulder as he spoke.

'Without a doubt,' Frog agreed. 'Nature is essential for good health, and good health a prerequisite for clear thinking. Mens sana in corpore sano.'

'Well spoken, master,' Crocs said. 'A fitting quotation. I trust you have both, today?'

'Thank you, dear Crocs. Yes, I am in good health and the clarity of my thinking is ready to be tested. What shall we discuss?'

Crocs looked again over his shoulder.

'I have some suggestions,' he said, 'as, most likely, do you. What are your offerings? Anything pressing?'

'Nothing that can't wait,' Frog said. 'Let's take one of yours. If you don't mind me saying so, you seem a little restless today.'

'Just a tad, perhaps,' Crocs admitted. 'It's a practical matter, more than anything. I have this feeling, now and again, that something is behind me. I can't actually hear anything, but I get the sensation that I'm hearing something, just a few steps away.'

Again, he looked over his shoulder.

'I can see that must be annoying,' Frog said. 'Any idea what it might be, or what could be causing it?'

'Not the slightest,' Crocs said, smiling now for having brought the matter up. 'I guess it's probably nothing more than my vivid imagination.'

'Mmm,' Frog said. 'Do you think it could be echoes from the past?'

'You mean like skeletons in the cupboard? Things I've done wrong, mistakes I've made, unprocessed emotions that have come to haunt me?'

'Forgive me, Crocs,' Frog said, hastily. 'Far be it from me to suggest any of that could be the case in your exemplary existence. I meant it more literally. Apparently, it's a natural phenomenon that happens sometimes. As you well know the present doesn't truly exist and is merely an abstract notion to indicate the now that we can never grasp, as the now has already slipped through our fingers and has become the past before we can even think the word 'now'. We can only look back to the past and — hopefully — forward to the future. I have read somewhere that, if one lives one's life intensely, it can happen that the present — unstoppable as it is — sometimes briefly reverberates behind us, as if to say that it doesn't want to leave us yet. I believe it's referred to as 'echoes from the past', although 'echoes from the present' would perhaps be more precise.'

'That's so interesting,' Crocs said.

'Indeed,' said Frog, 'and given how much you seem to be able to fit into your days, with your boundless energy and the inspiration you bring wherever you go, I wouldn't be in the least surprised if you heard the occasional echo behind you.'

'Thank you for your kind words,' Crocs said. 'But am I really so bad? It's not that I feel stressed or that my pulse is always racing. I'm just enjoying my life. Very much in fact! I look forward to it. I would hate to miss any moment of it.'

'Ah,' Frog replied. 'Hearing you speak in that way makes me think my diagnosis must be correct. Don't be alarmed. Such echoes can do no harm. On the contrary — they are nothing but tiny tickles; a happy little wave from a past present, as if to say, more of that, please. They're a good thing — definitely — but they can take a little while to get used to.'

'Do you have them, too?' Crocs asked.

'Indeed, I do, occasionally,' Frog said, 'but I would think I'm less at risk of hearing them than you are, for obvious reasons.'

They walked on in silence for a while. Crocs was mulling it all over, checking Frog's reasonable explanation against his recent experiences of the echoes from the past phenomenon — if, at least, that's what it was. Frog gave him the time he needed, noticing that, already, his friend no longer looked over his shoulder quite so often.

After a minute or ten, Crocs restarted their dialogue by asking what Frog made of the potential benefits of a silent retreat, as recently taken up by Fish. It was a considerate question. Crocs was aware how worried Frog had felt that afternoon of the search, and Frog, as brave and strong as he liked to portray himself, was thankful for the opportunity to relate his uneasy emotions once more.

After that they discussed many more subjects in elegant terms. Both were surprised how soon they arrived in the forest square, where they sat down for a brief repose. They both imagined hearing the happy echoes behind them, but at that moment, neither felt the urge to look back.

24   Going all the Way

'Mind out!' Hedgehog called out to Elephant from one of the lower branches over Beech Lane. 'Please keep the path clear!'

Before Elephant could even consider ignoring the red and white tape cordoning off a section of the lane and taking further steps upon it, Hedgehog had already jumped off her perch, slid with gusto onto a cleverly constructed slope of earth, and was gathering speed. Like a canon-ball her compactly balanced body shot along the track set out over a fair distance of the lane, a track which included further slopes catapulting the fearless protagonist high up in the air, funnels that sucked her up again and consequently accelerated her rounded body into a dizzying constellation of twists and turns until, finally, aided by a timely released parachute, she came to a screeching halt, no more than two feet away from Elephant's big toenail.

'Sorry to be shouting at you from a distance,' Hedgehog said, whilst undoing the parachute cords. 'I didn't want you to get hurt on the lane without knowing what had hit you.'

'I appreciate that,' Elephant said. 'I'm glad you warned me. Just in time, I think. I didn't realise what the red and white tape was there for.'

'Well, security, obviously,' Hedgehog explained. 'In the first place, I wouldn't like to pin myself in full flight onto unsuspecting passers-by like yourself, and, secondly, to stop any philistine senselessly modifying my carefully balanced trajectory, thereby compromising my personal safety.'

Elephant let his eyes glide over Hedgehog's track.

'Impressive set up,' he concluded. 'Is this installation permanent?'

'Only today and tomorrow,' Hedgehog explained. 'I have a licence. I needed to practice somewhere and, understandably, the Beech Lane committee granted me permission, in light of the international success I will be able to achieve.'

'I'm impressed,' Elephant said. 'You are certainly taking this very seriously. Very inspiring! What heights are you hoping to reach?'

'World Champion,' Hedgehog said. 'Nothing less! I must take things seriously! I want to go all the way. If you have a talent, you must use it or lose it, as they say.'

'Absolutely,' Elephant agreed. 'When did you discover that you were good at this? How long have you been training? By the way, don't let me stop your practice.'

But Hedgehog was more than pleased to take a short break and answer Elephant's questions. While she refolded her brake-chute in the correct manner, she told Elephant about her eureka moment, when she realised she had to have something that others admired her for; how Eagle had given her the idea when she told her that, from above, when Hedgehog had rolled herself up, she looked like a perfectly round stone, and how she had her first taste of performing on stage at Jay's show. Also, how she had been saving up for the right kit, slides and slopes, so that her training track would closely resemble the one used in official matches.'

'Incredible!' Elephant reiterated his growing admiration. 'No half measures! Your commitment to this sport is commendable. When are the championships?'

'It's art, actually, rather than sport,' Hedgehog corrected. 'Speed is important, but what matters more is the difficulty of the movement and the clarity of line. That's what the judges will be looking for. As for your last question — I'm hoping next summer. So far nothing has been scheduled yet but, as you just said yourself you thought I looked inspiring, I'm in no doubt that other competitors will take it up before long.'

'Most certainly,' Elephant said. 'I'd be surprised if they didn't. Well, thank you, Hedgehog, for telling me some of the background. Your talent will be hard to compete against.'

Elephant was about to move on and leave Hedgehog to start her next round of practice, but then he stopped and turned around.

'Hedgehog, listen,' he said. 'I have no other commitments this afternoon. I was just wondering if I could be of any assistance to you? You know, create some additional loops via my back and trunk. I'd like to be involved.'

Hedgehog was delighted with the offer. She immediately saw the possibilities and gave Elephant precise instructions on how to position himself for adding an even more challenging twist to the track. They practised for the rest of the afternoon and the whole of the next day, too. By the end of it, both Hedgehog and Elephant were convinced that any potential title contenders, if they even existed, would have some serious catching up to do.

25   Meaning Well

'Wouldn't you be better off starting at the other end?' Cyrus enquired. 'Seems to me that, if you work from right to left, you'd be less likely to miss it.'

'Not a bad suggestion,' Mole said, but she had no intention of changing her own approach for the one Cyrus suggested and disappeared back under the lawn to try again from left to right, which, in her humble opinion, made more sense.

But when she reappeared, five minutes later on the other side, without success, the smile on Cyrus's face grew bigger.

'No luck?' he asked.

'Nope,' Mole answered, trying to stay polite, whilst hoping that Cyrus would clear off to annoy someone else, somewhere else. Given time and patience she would be perfectly able to relocate her notebook by herself.

Alas — Cyrus seemed in no rush to vanish. In fact, even worse, Ladybird happened to pass by and sat down next to him.

'What's going on?' Ladybird asked. 'Has she lost something?'

'Her notebook,' Cyrus explained. 'Mole is expected at the meeting this afternoon, but she can't remember what she was supposed to look into, and now she's unable to look it up. She can't remember where she left it.'

'What a nuisance, Mole,' Ladybird said. 'But wouldn't you do better to go from right to left? I reckon that would reduce the risk of accidentally skipping over it.'

'Thank you for your considerations, Ladybird,' Mole said, 'but, if you don't mind, I prefer sticking to my own method.'

She walked over the lawn, back to the other side, where she went down under again, a yard away from her earlier search trajectory.

When, once again, she resurfaced at the end of the new line — sadly still without her notebook — Goat, Blackbird and Heron had joined the earlier onlookers. It had already been explained to them what was missing.

'Didn't you make a note of where you put it?' Blackbird asked. 'I always write down everything that I mustn't forget. My memory is so poor these days.'

Blackbird's friendly enquiry only rubbed more salt into the wound.

'I did,' Mole admitted, 'but — foolishly — in my notebook. I've never lost it before.'

'Happens to the best,' Heron said. 'If you hadn't lost it underground, I'd happily scan the lawn for you, but I'm afraid I can't help you below the surface. Even my vision has its limits. I agree with Ladybird, though, that from right to left might be more logical.'

'If you ask me,' Goat started, but by now Mole had reached boiling point and interrupted him rudely.

'I didn't ask you,' she said, 'and no, I don't need your help! Why don't you all just leave me in peace and go home? Why don't you all get out of my sight and consult your own notes for the meeting?'

Mole immediately went underground again. She didn't like blowing her top, but this time her well-meaning friends had driven her to the edge.

As for the friends, they realised they had gone too far. From the steam, rising up through the earth where Mole was continuing her search, they could tell that her anger wasn't going to be short-lived. It was probably best to do as she wished. They made sure not to be around when Mole resurfaced again.

Was it Mole's passionate outburst that inspired success? During her next thunderous and steaming march underground — from left to right — she suddenly felt the smooth soft leather of her notebook underneath her. Of course, she'd left it where she had taken yesterday's afternoon nap. She would have worked that out easily, if her pesky onlookers had left her more head-space to think about it. She dug herself a fresh exit there and then, enabling her to rise immediately, in triumph, and show her friends that her direction of search had been perfectly adequate. Unfortunately, just when she would have liked an audience, there was no longer one to be found.

Later however, some twenty minutes before the afternoon meeting started, Mole was already seated in her place. She'd had a brief preliminary chat with Owl, who usually chaired such gatherings, about her preferred course of action regarding certain matters on the agenda and, in general, the direction of travel that she thought their affairs should take. When the others arrived, they found Mole in a relaxed state of mind, tapping out some old jazz tune on the table, whilst drawing doodles in the margins of her notebook.

26   The Colour of the Sky

'Let's not beat about the bush,' Heron said. 'If you wish to get on in life, you must pay attention.'

Immediately, all who were gathered shifted in their seats and sat up straight. Heron's regimental style of speaking came as no surprise, nor did the beady eyes with which he gazed at his audience. It took a brave heart to ignore his display of seniority. But the presentation this afternoon was intended to be informative rather than authoritative, and Heron himself, having secured everyone's full attention, swiftly mellowed his message.

'Of course, one's eye for detail can be taken too far,' he went on, 'as my own, sometimes bitter experience has taught me but, nevertheless, observation is essential, dear friends. Close observation of the world around us holds the key to our success.'

He paused, took a sip of water, and then continued.

'Now, you may ask why I start talking about success and getting on in life, in a presentation which is entitled 'The Colour of The Sky'. Let me explain. Even the least observant of us will know that the colour of the sky doesn't exist. Yes, of course, we talk about a blue sky or a red sky, or even a pink one, but those are gross generalisations. If you look more precisely, and perhaps take a little more time for it, you'll soon discover that, for example, blue can have many different variations on different days, and that, even on one day, there is a huge array of colours in something we lazily summarise as being blue.'

Crocs and Frog, sitting next to each other in the front row, were nodding their heads in agreement.

'The world that surrounds us — that very beautiful world — is a complicated one and the rich colour palette that we find in the sky — in any sky and on any day — is there to remind us of that beauty. If, next, we look at the complexity of the greens, in trees, fields, shrubs or reeds, or at the myriad of colours we can detect in water, we understand a little better the enormous challenge of seeing all this accurately. It seems impossible, doesn't it? Yet, it doesn't stop there, because our world is also constantly in motion, sparkling, glistening, radiating. Indeed, the spectacle around us is absolutely dazzling and ever changing. That's what makes it so beautiful.'

Had there been some restlessness in the audience to begin with, by now everyone was completely mesmerized, absorbed by the way Heron made a story of something they all knew — somehow — had they taken time to think about it. And none of them had suspected that Heron, with his authoritative stare, was also an artist and poet, that his visionary skills had such a deep emotional undercurrent.

'I can tell that your heads are already buzzing,' Heron continued, 'and therefore, I will not delve into the even greater mysteries of sound and smell, that make our little paradise here even more complex and beautiful. Today I will stick to colours and movement. Now — and you may have already wondered this — why is it relevant to note all these colour variations and fluctuations? Why isn't it sufficient to call the sky blue, the grass green and the water wet?'

'On a very basic level the answer to these questions is simple. The accuracy of your observation will bring advantages, for example, it will tell you where to step and what ground to avoid, or it will tell you what kind of weather is due. Ladybird will, no doubt, support me in this. Precise observations will also help determine where best to fish, build, and perhaps even the best places to write poetry. And if we apply observational skills to our social life it will help us to note what our friends like and dislike, tell us when a compliment will do them good or when they would rather be left in peace, all of which is, of course, useful for building our friendships, or — to put it in more scientific terms — to be more socially effective.'

Again, Heron waited a little, to let the far-reaching consequences of his analysis sink in.

'However, advantageous as all that may be, it's still not the real crux of the matter. What we need to understand — what we must never forget — is that, always, we ourselves are at the centre of our observations. Everything you may see around you, every little detail you notice, is ever again a reflection of your own being. Our observations not only collect information about our surroundings — information we need to thrive and survive — but they also help us understand who we are and what our place is in the world. The better we observe what is around us, the better we will get to know ourselves. And the better we know ourselves, the better we will be able to get on, with ourselves..., and with one another. Therefore, dear friends, if I may conclude with a simple word of advice to send you on your way: always look up to the sky, pay attention to its colours — and see yourself!'

A thunderous applause followed, as Heron bowed

stiffly. Many stood up to express their admiration for the inspirational illumination of the craft of observation, that — clearly — Heron mastered so well. The enthusiastic response also expressed appreciation that Heron, mostly thought to be rigid and formal in his opinions, had so generously shared his depth of understanding, thereby cleverly not lecturing from afar, but bringing his message home by speaking about 'we' and 'our'. There were many questions to be answered, in particular about how one could improve one's skills in observation quickly, and Heron took time to answer everyone patiently.

Cyrus and Elephant had arrived late and slipped in at the back. Cyrus observed his friend, noting how he soaked up everything that Heron had said. It evidently impressed him.

27   Consternation

It was close to midnight, but Bull didn't feel in the least like sleeping. Not for the first time he thought that the world was beautiful. It was completely still; no wind, no sounds, apart from bits of a far-away conversation — probably between Owl and Moth — that drifted his way. The night had wrapped his field into a blanket of comfort, warm and secure around him. The night smells were amazing, so delicate and sweet, and, above him, the Stars in their millions were telling him how lucky he was to be alive.

Oh yes, it had been pointed out to him before, and by several of his friends, that he was a sentimental creature who always saw everything as being bright and beautiful. He had been mocked plenty of times for that and was told that, even if he were covered in mud, he would still consider himself to be blessed. It was true, so what was the point in denying it? What was wrong with being a soft soul, apart from the fact that this state of bliss often kept him awake, as it did tonight?

Bull decided to make the most of the wonderful night and go for a stroll towards the river. The Stars made it easy to see where he was going. Ahead of him they lit up the path, and they also tickled the smooth skin of the beech trees and made them look like a row of lanterns that seemed to say: Come this way, Bull, we'll take you to the river.

Reaching the waterfront, he immediately noticed Fish, who clearly was as sleepless as he was.

'Hey, Fish,' Bull said. 'Isn't it a beautiful night?

Everything is so still and perfect.'

Fish agreed.

'Indeed,' she said. 'Makes you happy to be alive, doesn't it?'

'It sure does,' Bull said.

Both felt that it wasn't necessary to say much more, that in many ways it was much better not to speak, not to drive the night magic away with words. For quite a while they both simply soaked up the wonderful state of being they experienced, augmented even more by knowing they were sharing it. But after some more time, Bull found it difficult to remain silent.

'Do you also have trouble sleeping on nights like this?' he asked.

'Yep,' Fish said. 'It's the Stars; their reflection in the water. Don't get me wrong, I'm not complaining about it. In fact, I love it. It's beautiful but, of course, it also creates a rather lively spectacle, which is not conducive to sleeping.'

Bull thought the twinkling of the Stars on the river was mesmerizing. He looked up to the mystery in the sky.

'Quite a consternation up there,' he said.

'Don't you mean a constellation?' said Fish.

'No, I mean the Stars,' Bull said. 'The consternation of the Stars above us that cause the waves to twinkle so beautifully.'

'It's called a constellation,' Fish said. 'A constellation of stars is the correct phrase.'

'Are you sure?' Bull asked. 'Owl told me it was a consternation.'

'You must have misheard,' Fish said. 'Owl would

never get something like that wrong.'

There was nothing more Bull could say to that. Fish seemed convinced that she was right, as he himself could now no longer be. He distinctly remembered Owl talking, two or three weeks ago, about the consternation up there, but Owl wasn't here now to clarify matters, so Bull couldn't take the debate any further, neither did he want to.

Fish and Bull stayed together for another ten minutes, again not saying anything but taking in the magic. At least, they were trying to. When Bull felt that enough quiet time had gone by, he made his excuses.

'I think I'll make another attempt at falling asleep,' he said. 'As beautiful as all of this is, I guess, at a certain time we have to surrender.'

But back at his field he was further away from sleeping than ever. Fish's last remark - 'getting something like that wrong' - was still ringing in his ears. It was hurtful. Did Fish think he was stupid? Consternation or constellation, what difference did it make? Fish had really no need to ruin his mood over such a tiny matter. He would ask Owl at a suitable time what it should be and — in the case that Fish was right — why Owl had misinformed him.

With those thoughts in his mind sleep finally took him off. He had a few hours left before dawn came but those hours were not all that restorative.

Half an hour into the new day, however, Bumblebee appeared.

'Message from Fish,' she said. 'She's asking if you'll join him for breakfast. I think she's feeling bad. I'm not sure what about.'

28   The Facts of Life

Blackbird, Mole, Bumblebee and Frog were gathered around the table at Frog's. Each had brought a small object and placed it on the table in front of them. Frog had poured everyone a drink and had lit the big candle in the middle of the table to create extra atmosphere.

'Right,' said Bumblebee, 'what are we doing? I haven't played this before. What do you want us to do?'

'Let me explain,' said Frog. 'It's a game that can be played in a lighthearted way but, as you will see, it can also be taken more seriously. I have asked you to bring something — the objects that we have here in front of us — that has a special meaning to you. They are important to us, for one reason or another. Our task in this game is to tell the story about your object. What you tell us must to be true and we can ask questions about it. Does that make sense?'

The other three nodded.

'Brilliant,' Frog said. 'To begin, I also have to say a couple of introductory lines, to set the tone as it were. Here we go.'

He stretched out his front legs and took hold of Bumblebee's on the left and Mole's on the right, indicating to Blackbird opposite him that he had to do the same and complete the circle. And when they were all connected, Frog spoke slowly in a theatrical voice.

'Dear Friends. I welcome you to my table. Thank you for gathering in my home and bringing gifts. Together we shall investigate the facts of life. Together we shall follow the threads woven into the cloth of the world and rejoice in the stories they will tell us. Master Blackbird, please reveal your gift.'

'I have brought a feather,' Blackbird said, 'but I hadn't understood it had to be a gift. I will need to use this again.'

'Of course,' Frog said. 'Don't worry about the gift thing, that's only metaphorically speaking, just to set the tone.'

'Oh, good,' Blackbird said.

'Master Blackbird,' Frog repeated, 'please reveal your gift to us.'

'Well,' Blackbird said, 'as you can see, I've brought a feather. It's a black feather, but it's not one of mine. Can you guess what's special about it?'

The others shook their heads.

'Is it for flying long distance?' Frog tried. 'Does it tell you how far from home you are?'

'Not quite,' Blackbird said. 'This feather was given to me by my father, and he was given it by his father, and I think it has been in the family for much longer even. It's my special composition feather. I use it for penning down my melodies. I guess you all think that I'm just improvising my songs, don't you?'

They all nodded.

'Well, I don't. A lot of hard work goes into those tunes. There are always so many options but, of course, they don't all hit the spot, and this feather helps me to get the balance right. It's musically charged. I'll pass it on to my children one day.'

Mole, Frog and Bumblebee gasped as one. They had no idea of the skill that was involved in what they had always thought were spontaneous outbursts from their musical friend.

The game continued.

'Mistress Bumblebee,' Frog started, but then he stopped and said that Blackbird ought to do the next one.

'Mistress Bumblebee,' Blackbird said, copying Frog's theatrical voice as well as he could, 'please reveal your gift to us.'

Bumblebee had brought a tiny snuffbox, in which she carried twelve different flower powders.

'These are the very best,' she explained, 'twelve fragrances, that hold the key to everything you might smell among the flowers. Occasionally I come across something that I have not seen or tried before, but with this box of classic samples I can always determine their class and origin. It's the art of compare and contrast, I suppose. I also use this set to recalibrate my own sense of smell now and again, when I've had too much pollen up my nose and my sensors have become a little overheated.'

Mole, who came next, had brought what she called her turn stone, a highly polished grey pebble with a white line straight through the middle, which she used for her orientation underground. Whenever she entered certain tunnels that needed maintenance or that she hadn't visited for a while, she placed the turn stone at a junction, as an anchor point for all underground calculations she might have to make. It also helped remind her of the way she had come.

Finally, Frog showed his friends an oak twig that was very smooth and dark.

'It must have been in the water for decades,' he explained. 'I found it last summer, lodged under one of my lily pads. It really felt as if it had come to find me. I have used it ever since, at least twice a day, for all my stretches and jumping exercises. I have to keep my muscles supple, you see.'

In this way they told each other anecdotes from their lives, at first hearing perhaps of little significance, but after some consideration absolutely at the very heart of their existence. And, somehow, those stories locked into each other. They all related to the simple secrets that made a success and a pleasure of their days.

At the end of the evening Frog once more put on his theatrical voice to end the game.

'Dear friends,' he said, with all of them joining the circle again, 'we have learned this evening about the facts of life. Fellow masters and mistresses of this world, with a warm heart I thank you for enlightening our evening with the gift of your stories. We now know one another, and we will remain connected, forevermore. Thank you.'

After these special words Mole, Bumblebee and Blackbird each took their 'gifts' and made their way back home, but not before thanking Frog for his hospitality. They all knew it had been an evening that they would never forget.

29   Being in Denial

'You're going grey, aren't you?' said Crocs to Owl, with a big, cheeky smile on his face. 'Are your years of wisdom finally catching up with you?'

Owl was taken aback.

'Trick of the light,' she said, rather sternly. 'I've always had grey amongst my feathers. I'm surprised you've never noticed that before.'

In Crocs' eyes Owl most definitely looked a little older than she did last week and, as far as he was concerned, that was no big deal.

'None of us are getting any younger, are we?' he said. 'I'm definitely not as fit as I used to be but I tell myself that a bit of wear and tear or a little extra ballast only makes us more beautiful.'

He patted his belly, which was, indeed, considerably rounder than in earlier days, and grinned, but he should have realised he was taking a risk. With his last comment he had overstepped the mark. Owl wasn't smiling.

'It appears you have more talent for self-indulgence than for being respectful regarding other's appearances. It might serve you well to apply more personal control and hope that it will improve your manners and your shape, before it's too late.'

She still wasn't smiling. It was Crocs' turn to be taken aback by Owl taking this so seriously. Best leave it and change the subject, he thought.

'You're right, of course, as always.' (A little flattery would perhaps help Owl to relax). 'Hey, have you heard how well Hedgehog is progressing with her new sport, or art, as she calls it? She's training seriously hard.'

But Owl wasn't letting Crocs off the hook.

'She's a disciplined little character,' Owl said, 'someone who doesn't like to let things slip.'

Later that afternoon, back at home, Dragonfly dropped by. Crocs was pleased with the distraction. He hadn't been able to put the stiff conversation with Owl out of his mind and couldn't decide if he'd been in the wrong and should go back to apologise, or if he should ignore Owl's uncalled-for brusqueness. His remark had been nothing but innocent and playful. If Owl was unable to take it light-heartedly, then that was her problem. But the thing kept playing on his mind.

'Drinks?' he asked.

'If you have time,' said Dragonfly. 'That would be lovely.'

Crocs poured them both a glass and they sat down together on his veranda to enjoy the sunshine.

'How are things with you?' Crocs enquired. He wondered if Dragonfly had noticed his round belly, but there was nothing he could do about that right now, other than perhaps sitting up properly.

'I'm fine,' Dragonfly said, 'but I just had this awkward conversation with Owl. I happened to say that her grey feathers look rather dashing, but she took it completely the wrong way, told me I was colour-blind, and that I should go and see a doctor about my nervous disposition. I only tried to compliment her on how well she is maturing, in my eyes, at least.'

'That's funny,' Crocs said. 'Well, not that funny, really. I had a similar conversation with Owl this morning.'

Crocs was about to tell Dragonfly about his own

exchange with Owl, but then Frog turned up.

'Thank goodness,' Frog said. 'At last, some civilised beings. May I join you? I've just been to see Owl and, before I could even open my mouth, she told me to 'hop off', because she didn't have time for any of my rudeness.'

'Did you by any chance comment on her feathers going grey?'

'No way,' said Frog. 'I had even brought her a cake, but I didn't give it to her, not after she talked to me like that. I mean, what kind of welcome is that? I did notice, though. She's looking older, isn't she?'

Tucking into Frog's cake, the three of them agreed that Owl was beginning to show her age. In many ways it was a relief that they could lay the matter at Owl's feet. They had all noticed it — Owl looking more grey — but, clearly, it was a sensitive matter for her.

'You'd think that if any of us should be proud of our ripe old age it would be Owl,' Frog said.

'That's what I tried to tell her,' Crocs said, 'that there's nothing wrong with getting older, even when it shows.'

He wondered if Frog noticed his belly.

'She's in denial,' Dragonfly said. 'She doesn't want to know.'

Dragonfly seemed to have hit the nail on the head.

'So, what do we do now?' Frog asked. 'Just wait until this blows over, until Owl is in a better mood again?'

'That could take quite a while,' Crocs said.

They sipped their drinks, trying to work out a strategy

for changing things around.

'I wonder,' Dragonfly said, after a while. 'Perhaps we have to find a way to make being older and grey seem attractive. If you ask me, Owl is in denial because she's worried that she may be losing her looks. We have to make maturity desirable.'

'Easier said than done,' Crocs said. 'How do you suggest we achieve that?'

But Dragonfly was a creative thinker, and a plan was already forming in her mind.

'Here's an idea,' she said. 'We place an ad in the paper calling for a mature lady of age with grey locks.'

'Like a dating ad?' Frog asked.

'I thought more along the lines of an audition for a play,' said Dragonfly. 'Something in which Owl could play the leading part.'

'Mrs Marple?' Frog suggested.

'Excellent idea,' said Crocs.

Crocs got paper and pen and they spent the rest of the afternoon working out details. They had to get the text for the advert exactly right, for Owl to recognise her own profile and her potential for the role, and simultaneously make her realise that her 'greying' was the one quality that made her stand out from the crowd and would get her the part. Someone else would need to take charge of the auditioning process, to avoid Owl becoming suspicious. They thought maybe Cyrus and Peacock would do it.

The cunning plan worked to perfection. In fact, it soon turned out to be a lot of fun. Cyrus and Peacock were dead keen, and Peacock also wished to direct the play. Others became involved too. Moth was tasked with making sure Owl got to see the advert.

Owl took the bait. She signed up for the auditions. Dragonfly auditioned too, but that was, of course, a set-up, only so that she could congratulate Owl for getting the part.

'They didn't think I was mature enough to play Mrs Marple,' she explained to Owl. 'They thought I lacked gravitas.'

The play was a huge success, not in the least because Owl adopted her character brilliantly and truly starred as the clever detective. Frog had accepted a small part. Dragonfly and Crocs kept themselves off stage but made sure not to miss any of the scheduled performances. They couldn't help giggling, every time they heard Mrs Marple, with her voice of mature authority, address the other actors with the lines: 'Ah, but we can be certain of deceit and that a crime is already unfolding, right here under our noses. We only have to face the facts.'

30   Lucky Day

It was only a moment, but things could have turned out very differently for Dragonfly, if she hadn't been able — in the nick of time — to pull herself up steeply. Had she been dreaming in full flight, or had she been distracted, trying to recall the poem that Moth read to her last night? In any case, only at the very last moment did she avoid crashing into a nasty old rock sticking out above the water, which would have left her severely hurt. She escaped with the shakes only. She landed on a branch reaching out over the river and tried to regain control of herself.

Fish popped up nearby.

'Everything alright?' she asked.

'Fine, thanks,' Dragonfly answered. 'Near miss. I must have been dozing off. Didn't look where I was going.'

'Happens to the best,' Fish said in a voice of comfort. 'I'm glad you're ok. It must be your lucky day.'

'Yes, fortunately,' Dragonfly said.

When the shock of her near miss had receded and her thoughts of what could have happened ebbed away, Dragonfly decided she would visit Bull. Bull always had a calming influence on her. For one reason or another, Bull's unquestioning state of being made things feel right. Dragonfly loved being in his company.

But just as she left the forest, the old Oak Tree overlooking Bull's field dropped nine or ten acorns at once. Suddenly, Dragonfly found herself mid-air in a shower of acorn canon-balls and she had to use all her navigation skills to find a clear passage through and survive the unsolicited assault unscathed.

'Thanks a lot,' she said to the Oak Tree. 'Can't you watch what you're doing?!'

'I'm sorry, sweetheart,' the Oak Tree said. 'I hadn't expected you here at this time of day. I've got to drop them sometime, but it wasn't my intention to hurt you.'

'Well, I'm glad you didn't,' Dragonfly said. 'You could have squashed me. Hope you'll take more care next time.'

But the Oak Tree didn't appreciate being talked to in that way.

'I've said I'm sorry, sweetie,' he said, 'but it's you who should look better where you're going. If you choose to take a shortcut through my space without warning me you can't hold me responsible.'

Dragonfly didn't waste time arguing with the careless assailant. Things seemed to be conspiring against her today. Perhaps she'd do better to go home and stay put, but, by now, she was already so close to Bull's field.

'Two near misses, you say?' Bull asked. 'It must be your lucky day.'

'That's what Fish said after the first one,' Dragonfly said. 'I guess it depends how you look at it. You could just as well conclude that, twice, I almost was very unlucky. Anyway, enough of that. What have you been up to, lately?'

They chatted about this and that, and the medicine of Bull's presence soon took effect. Dragonfly calmed down. Hadn't Owl accused her of being too nervy, a while ago? Perhaps she should take things a bit slower. She was always skipping from one place to the other, never completely satisfied, always feeling she should move on. How much easier life must be if one was like Bull, happy to be in his field, without the need to be flitting about. Even when he just lifted his head or tail, Bull took his time to do it. Dragonfly couldn't remember ever seeing Bull startled.

Her friend interrupted her thoughts.

'Going back to what we said earlier...,' Bull said. 'I've heard it said that being lucky is making sure to be prepared when an opportunity comes along.'

'That's a new one to me,' said Dragonfly, 'but I can subscribe to it. Maybe that's why I always try to be in more than just one place at once.'

'Ah, but it goes further than that,' Bull said. 'There's always an element of adventure in new opportunities. You need to be in a fit mental state to take on new challenges.'

Dragonfly was thinking it over.

'I think it would be good to look at your day as an adventure,' Bull continued. 'Both times your reflexes were perfect. You were well prepared. Yes, on balance I would say that calling yourself 'lucky' is more fitting than saying you were 'almost unlucky'.'

When Dragonfly returned home, she was in a much better place. Bull's personality was a panacea for her hyperactive disposition and her friend had given her much food for thought. So much in fact that, again, she wasn't fully concentrating and almost had all the air knocked out of her by Hedgehog and her never-ending deathly sky loops that she now practised in the weirdest places. Dragonfly managed to scoop past Hedgehog with only the breadth of a whisker between them. Hedgehog hadn't even seen her. Dragonfly didn't bother giving her a mouthful.

'Third time lucky,' was all she thought.

31   Point of View

'Can you see that cloud over the brow of the hill?' said Beetle. From where I sit, that looks just like a lion.'

'What does a lion look like?' Fish wanted to know.

'Have you never seen a lion?' Beetle asked.

'Have you?'

'Only in a picture,' Beetle admitted. 'Owl showed me one in a book a while ago.'

Just at that moment Owl herself happened to swoop by. Fish called out to her.

'Owl, do you have a moment? Beetle is trying to explain to me what a lion looks like. He says that cloud resembles one. Can you confirm that?'

Owl studied the cloud, that had, by now, moved a short distance and had also stretched itself out a little.

'I think I can go along with Beetle,' she said, diplomatically, 'at least, partially. It's not easy to see from this distance, and my knowledge is, of course, only second hand. Hard to say. There's some resemblance, but if you want exact verification I would speak to Elephant. I know for a fact that he has seen lions close up.'

Beetle and Fish both thought that was a good idea.

'You might be in luck,' Owl added. 'I just saw Elephant heading to Hippo's new place. Perhaps you'll catch them both. I'd be surprised if Hippo didn't also have a lion memory, or two.'

Fish swam upriver to where Hippo lived, whilst Beetle flew over the water, which he thought was exhausting, but a sacrifice worth making for proving his point. If Elephant and Hippo did, indeed, have first-hand experience of lions, they would, no doubt, be able to validate his observation instantly as a correct one.

Luck was on their side. The two found Elephant and Hippo at the waterfront end of Hippo's lawn, having a convivial exchange of jokes and anecdotes. Fish addressed them.

'Afternoon,' she said. 'Forgive us for dropping in on you without notice. We'd like to ask your opinion, if we may.'

'Of course,' Elephant said. 'How may we help?'

'Beetle wants to show me what a lion looks like, and he says that the cloud over there looks just like a lion. Owl has told us you are experts on the matter. Do you both think that cloud looks like a lion?'

Hippo and Elephant simultaneously looked up to the cloud that Fish pointed at. Unfortunately, the cloud had, again, moved further and it was now also partly obscured by a big tree. Only its rear end was still visible.

'What's your opinion?' Elephant asked Hippo.

Hippo read the situation well and understood that Beetle's credibility was at stake.

'From what I can see it's a convincing case,' she said. 'The back end certainly looks right, with that tail-piece there, but to say for sure you would need to see the front part as well. You can only truly tell a lion by its mane. Sadly, I can't see that bit from here. The cloud is travelling in the right direction, though. Southwards. That's where most lions live.'

Beetle's hopes, briefly raised by Hippo's first words, were dashed again. But Elephant had a good suggestion.

'Why don't you ask Eagle?' he said. 'Eagle always has a perfect point of view. She could fly around the cloud, look at it from all sides and give you a 360-degree assessment. I suppose that would be too big a task for you to undertake yourself.'

Indeed, it would. The idea of it already made Beetle shiver. Asking Eagle made complete sense.

They called out for her and very soon Eagle joined the company. When they explained the issue, she was immediately happy to help. The cloud had again moved a little further, but that was no problem. Eagle could easily catch it up, fly around it and take a good look at it from all sides.

Half an hour later Eagle returned. By now, everyone was curious to hear the verdict.

'Definitely,' Eagle said as she landed. 'I had to dig deep into my own memory to remember what a lion looks like, but I thought there was a strong resemblance and then I just asked the Cloud directly. It almost got cross with me. 'Of course,' it said. 'Can't you tell? Don't you think I've made a brilliant job of looking like a lion?'

'Excellent! That, then, settles the matter,' Beetle said, proud and relieved. They all looked up to the sky once more, but by now the cloud had almost disappeared out of sight. Only the brush on the end of its tail was still visible.

32 Turmoil

Mole woke up in the middle of the night. She only realised that it was still night when she stepped outside for fresh air and noticed that it was pitch dark. Strange, she said to herself. She had always been a regular sleeper. What could have made her get up so early today or, more accurately, tonight?

Not finding an answer to this question, she went back to her bed, but as soon as she lay down, she felt a shudder coming from the earth beneath her dwelling. She sat up and observed the tremors travelling through all parts of her domain, like a wave coming onto the shore, first climbing and curling up, then collapsing and dispersing in a broad sway towards the land. That earth-wave must be what had woken her up.

She lay down again but almost immediately another shudder started, and after that another one.

'Hey, Earth, what's going on?' she said. 'I hope you're not going to quake on me and ruin my costly infrastructure?'

'I'll try not to,' said the Earth. 'It's just that I have this itch and I can't seem to get rid of it. My apologies for the disturbance. I hope it will go soon. In the meantime I'll do my best to endure it.'

But the itch didn't go, and the Earth didn't quite manage to control himself. It was Mole who had to endure. She lay awake for hours, thinking only of the mountain of clearing up work that she would have to face. She was glad when, at long last, the morning arrived.

Mole wasn't the only one who stepped outside for the second time that morning.

'Did you have a rotten night too?' Worm asked her straight away.

'Tell me about it,' said Mole. 'It was the Earth. He was plagued by an itch, quite seriously, I believe.'

And, as if to illustrate how right Mole was about the severity of the itch, the Earth shuddered again. In fact, the upheaval below them continued until mid-day.

In the afternoon Mole and Worm both managed to get on top of things; debris cleared where they had found it and furniture put back into place. Those tasks had been waiting to be done, anyway.

'I still think we should report this to Owl,' Mole said. 'It was probably just a one-off occurrence but, nevertheless, it ought to be logged.'

Worm agreed. They went over to Owl's place and told her about their restless night and the cause of it. Owl drew the same conclusion.

'Probably just a one-off,' she said, 'but prudent to get it onto the register. Thank you for reporting it.'

That evening Mole and Worm, both exhausted after the sleepless night and a hard day's work, went to bed early. Unfortunately, the earth had another itch that night, one no less ignorable than the previous time. On the contrary, it turned out to be much worse. This second itch went on for much longer into the next day, and when the clouds saw it, they, too, started itching. They became turbulent, twisting and turning with sharp and sudden outbursts of rain, that were a nuisance for Eagle and Bumblebee, although others like Frog and Blackbird didn't mind it too much.

In the afternoon, when — thank goodness — things calmed down again, Owl took in the new reports from Worm and Mole, as well as those from Eagle and Bumblebee.

'How likely is that?' she wondered. 'Unrest in the earth and turbulence in the clouds at the same time. I believe they call that a freak event, something that is unlikely to happen frequently.'

Her words, meant to ease concerns, only partially succeeded in their mission. Eagle, Bumblebee, Worm and Mole all went home with heavy hearts. They told themselves that the turmoil would pass, sooner or later, and they just hoped it would be sooner, rather than later.

Alas! The itch was not only stubborn and infectious, but also energetic and greedy. Bang on the next midnight hour it made its presence felt again, and whilst the earth and the sky, and everyone living in between, were bracing themselves for another rocky night, the turmoil became more aggressive by the minute, shaking the trees in the forest more violently than was enjoyable and filling the riverbed with more water than it appreciated.

The next day, at daybreak, it seemed there was hardly any point in clearing up the mess, at least, not before the commotion of earth and sky came to a halt. Instead, everyone fought their way through the blistering storm towards Owl. She was the only one who still had some mental capacity to offer comfort.

Under Owl's oak tree the crowd of animals huddled together, desperately wishing that the pandemonium would be over soon. But they heard the storm winds laugh out loud, saying, 'This is fun!', and they heard the oak tree groan, and they could only hope that it wouldn't start throwing its branches down on them.

'Stay close together,' Owl shouted. 'It will pass. Moments such as this have come to test us. We must show what we're made off. Think good things! Think about sunshine.'

How lucky they were to have Owl's unwavering courage and determination to cling to!

Was it their collective thinking that finally drove the storm away, that got rid of the itch and restored the much-desired calm? Was it their connected souls that brought the sun back out to warm their hearts and bones?

Soon everyone was busying themselves again, sorting out their business and bringing their lives back into order. Soon the recent turmoil was, indeed, classified as a freak event, a memory to be stored in their collective past. But it took Owl longer to find back her confidence in nature. Could she tell anyone how scared and defeated she had felt at that moment of ultimate uncertainty, when everyone looked towards her for strength, but everything was out of her control?

33   The River Belongs to Everyone

'We'd be so much better off if we all stuck to our own patch of river,' Heron said, under his breath and therefore to no one in particular. He stared at the riverbank on the other side, where Crocs, Hippo, Frog and Fish were all busying themselves with this or that, thereby constantly getting in each other's way. And, as if there weren't enough of them yet, Dragonfly also entered the scene and, evidently, felt the need to be as much on top of all the others as she could possibly be.

Goat happened to walk nearby and hear all of Heron's words clearly. As a matter of fact, he thought Heron was talking to him.

'But the river belongs to everyone, doesn't it?' he replied.

Heron was a little startled to find Goat so nearby. He gathered that Goat had heard what he had said to himself and now he had to weigh up quickly what strategy would serve him best; making out that Goat had misheard him and pretend not to understand his response; or have a go at him with the full force of his unrivalled authority. As Goat had the reputation of being a walkover, the choice was easy.

'That, my dear friend, is a matter of opinion,' Heron said. 'In your case, unsubstantiated opinion, if you don't mind me saying it as it is. Don't get me wrong; I'm no stranger to the socialist view about the river starting elsewhere and coming to us all equally, and all such wishful thinking, but that doesn't account for the reality that, once it has arrived in our world, the rules have significantly changed. Here, we all have our own patch, we look after our own bit of river, which we use for our personal needs. We have a vested interest and, therefore, the right to claim it as our own, don't you think?'

Heron accentuated his last three words, patronisingly spelling out that he didn't think much of Goat's thinking. Goat, however, had done a lot of thinking lately, and one of the conclusions he had reached was that he ought to do something about his reputation of being soft.

'Forgive me, Heron,' he said. 'You may regard the socialist doctrine a negligible perspective, but I beg to differ. In fact, I disagree strongly! Looking after something does not automatically make one its proprietor. I, for example look after my hoofs and horns — of course, I do — and I may freely claim their ownership, but I also look after the heather where I live, which is there for all to enjoy.'

Heron felt a little shocked by Goat's unexpected, firm assertion. He now realised he shouldn't underestimate the bearded fellow but, instead, sharpen his own argument.

'Enjoyment is not the point,' he said. 'Naturally, the sun shines and the birds sing, for all to enjoy — or not, as the case may be — but one shouldn't confuse enjoyment with responsibility. If our whole world were a free-for-all, it would lead to nothing but chaos. I salute you for the excellent results you, no doubt, achieve with your shrubbery, but you wouldn't want me interfering with that, would you? I know nothing about that kind of thing. In the same fashion, I wouldn't like to see you troubling my water or, at least, my patch of it, because I assume you have little knowledge of river management.'

Goat, who felt he had, so far, done well holding his

ground, stiffened his resolve.

'I don't disagree with your last assumption, Heron,' he said, 'but I must insist that you are missing the point — completely. You speak about being responsible, but the underlying case I hear you make, is one for your private needs and your personal satisfaction. Can you not see the greater good that we all work for, but need to work for together? Sharing the world is not simply about dividing it up into a share for each. It is as much about being together — caring, enjoying, collaborating — as it is about taking responsibility!'

'Lofty words, Goat,' Heron replied immediately. 'Look at those fools there, over on the other side. No doubt, they're all on your side of the argument. Do you see them taking responsibility? Look at them! From where I stand, one can only conclude that all they care for is that single, leisurely patch of river, with not a worry for any of the rest of it. Utter chaos! And why? Because no one is looking at the bigger picture. That 'greater good' that you talk about is an illusion. Nobody cares about it. None of them there even know what it is. They don't look any further than the end of their noses.'

Goat sensed Heron's anger, or something similar, something primeval. He wondered if he should have found someone else on whom to try out his new resolution of not being soft. On the other hand, he was still standing, wasn't he? Perhaps it was time to take another approach.

'Those fools, Heron,' he said, 'are our friends.'

He spoke softly, but he felt the authority in his voice. Where did that come from?

It seemed to work. Heron mellowed.

'I know,' he said. 'Of course, they are our friends. I didn't mean it like that.'

They stood side by side, both observing the scene on the other side of the river. Chaotic it was, indeed, but not lacking in enjoyment, and at least the playful group all cared for one another.

After a while, it was Goat who spoke again.

'Heron,' he said, 'do you care about the greater good? Do you know what it is?

'Of course, I do,' Heron said. 'Well, I have some idea of it. But, of course, I care about it.'

'In that case,' Goat said, 'can we try something? How about you look after my patch for a while, and I look after yours? Only for a couple of hours, or so. I promise I won't change anything without asking you first. Just to see if we can catch a glimpse of the bigger picture?'

'Your patch?' Heron asked.

'You know what I mean,' said Goat.

'Fine,' said Heron. He smiled.

'Let's try it.'

34   Noble Intentions

'I've been thinking about what you said, a while back,' Crocs said to Owl. 'You were right. I should do something about this.'

He patted his belly, which had again grown a little rounder than it had been last month.

'Noble intentions,' Owl said, 'but I wouldn't worry too much. You don't look so bad, do you? We all change with the years.'

'But last time you accused me of not having enough self-control?'

Owl didn't like being reminded of that tricky episode in their friendship.

'Did I? There's nothing wrong with that, is there? You're not one to let things get out of hand.'

Crocs struggled to work out Owl's response, as friendly as it was, this time. That last time, Owl had been in denial of her own maturing process, and everyone had successfully conspired to make her feel better about herself. Now she seemed to be in denial of having been in denial. Just when Crocs had hoped for sympathy and moral support from his friend, Owl simply waved his concerns away.

'So, you don't think I should try to lose weight?'

'That's up to you,' Owl said. 'If it makes you feel better, why not? What will you do? More exercise?'

Walking back, Crocs found himself in two minds. On the one hand, he was quite ready to have his concerns put to bed by Owl's light-hearted dismissal. Perhaps he was worrying about nothing. On the other hand, he couldn't deny being out of breath right now. He couldn't deny that even this short walk took him more effort than it used to, and that, recently, he had felt a lot more self-aware during social engagements. 'Noble intentions,' Owl had mocked, when all he had wanted was a little encouragement to face reality and deal with it.

Caught up in thoughts like these, Crocs hadn't noticed Goat coming from behind and catching up with him.

'Fabulous day,' Goat said. 'Apologies, I'm in a hurry. Can't slow down.'

Half a minute later Goat was out of sight again.

'Right,' Crocs said to himself. 'That's it. I'll have to take action. I'll show them all how noble my intentions really are.'

Back home, he made a list of the changes he would make to lose weight and regain fitness:

> *take smaller breakfasts*
> *cake only once a day*
> *half an hour exercise in the morning*
> *salad for lunch more often*
> *afternoon walks — every day*
> *no drinks before 5pm*
> *maximum 3 drinks per day*
> *no snacking*

He reviewed his action points. 'Formidable, but achievable,' he concluded. 'I'll start tomorrow.'

He wrote 'noble intentions' at the top of his list and pinned it to the wall, clearly visible, so that he would be reminded of his new self-discipline every time he walked past.

Crocs had agreed with himself that he would review the measures after a week. When that first week had finally gone by, he concluded that he'd done pretty well. He had enjoyed the morning exercise and the afternoon walks, and he felt he was already getting fitter. No snacking had been the most challenging. He had sinned maybe two or three times on that score and, also; he had received visitors a couple of times on sunny afternoons and felt it would have been rude not to offer them a little glass of something, even before 5pm. But, overall, he hadn't done badly, although, sadly, his belly did not yet show that his noble intentions were bearing fruit.

To get visible results he probably had to 'up' his game. So far, the new regime had not been too challenging. If he wanted to tighten his belt sooner, he should, perhaps, also raise his ambitions, if only fractionally.

But he didn't belief in half measures, so he replaced 'cake once a day' with 'no more cake', he crossed out 'more often' after 'salad', changed '3 drinks' to '2 drinks' and underlined 'no snacking'.

In that following week he followed his self-inflicted rules more strictly. It was tough, and not exactly what you'd call fun, but he knew there was too much at stake; not only his future fitness and better shape but also his self-esteem hung in the balance. Even when Hippo and Frog dropped by on Wednesday, as they often did, he made them wait until five before he offered them anything at all, and he only poured half-full glasses.

By the end of the week, he felt much better. He

was definitely fitter and his self-esteem had gloriously survived the more stringent measures. Unfortunately, so had his belly. It showed no signs of caving in. At least, not yet.

Crocs was disappointed but not defeated.

'Right,' he said to his belly, 'if you want to play hard, we'll play hard. I'll show you who's boss.'

On his list he crossed out lunch altogether, doubled his exercise time to two hours a day and, after some hesitation, also crossed out 'before 5pm' after 'no drinks', as well as the following line, which he now didn't need anymore.

It took two more weeks for his belly to finally surrender, and after that, another four weeks for it to have diminished to a size that, Crocs thought, was becoming acceptable. Sadly, there had been side-effects, too, most notably the departure of his usual smile and jovial manner. Crocs had hardly noticed himself that he had become rather serious. His mind was always taken up by what was allowed and what wasn't, and by the importance of fully committing to his noble intentions. He hadn't even noticed that no friends had dropped by for a while. Everybody was probably busy facing their own challenges.

Once Crocs was satisfied that he had come to where he wanted to be, belly-wise, he decided to pay Owl another visit.

'Goodness me, you've lost weight,' Owl observed.

'And feeling a lot better for it.'

'Haven't seen you for such a long time,' said Owl. 'Everything alright?'

'Absolutely,' Crocs said. 'It's so much better to feel in control, to be fit again, and not let things slip, as you said I did.'

Owl couldn't remember ever having said that, but she was pleased that Crocs was so positive and upbeat.

'I must say, it's a remarkable achievement,' said Owl. 'Congratulations. I feel we should celebrate. Drinks?'

Crocs' first thought was that it wasn't even lunch time yet.

'Go on then,' he said.

And, cautiously, the beginnings of his famous broad smile started curling his lips once more.

35   What We Don't Know

Usually, Bumblebee wasn't one for staying up late, but tonight an uncomfortable feeling of unease stopped her from settling down and even considering closing her eyes. Instead, she decided to visit Goat. Some said that Goat was no longer a melancholic, lost soul, but that he was quickly making a name for himself as being the opposite: a rock, a pillar of the community. Bumblebee hoped that, perhaps, Goat might lend her comfort.

Goat welcomed her heartily.

'What an absolute delight to see you,' he said, 'but isn't this a late hour for you to be out and about? To what do I owe the pleasure of your visit?'

It seemed to be true; Goat had changed. The sparkle in his eyes and his self-assured way of speaking resembled nothing of his old romantic self. Bumblebee immediately felt herself relaxing.

'Thank you, Goat,' she said. 'I needed to see someone and thought, as I haven't visited for a while, I'd see if you were at home. Is it convenient?'

'More than,' Goat said. 'As I said: a pleasure. Tell me what I can do to help. Are you not feeling well?'

'I don't know,' Bumblebee said. 'I'm fine. I mean, there's nothing wrong with me. It's just that I felt so apprehensive tonight — I don't even know why. I'm sorry, I shouldn't have come here and troubled you with it.'

'That,' Goat said, 'should be the least of your concerns. If friends can't be called upon in uncertain times, then what would be the point of friendship? We should take comfort from knowing that we're not alone.'

Bumblebee agreed, gratefully. Goat was right. They weren't alone. Sitting here side by side and staring into the dark night was already so much better. After a while she said:

'Do you sometimes ask yourself what's out there in the dark?'

'Very often,' Goat said. 'There aren't many stars out tonight, but when they're all sparkling it's even more mysterious, don't you think?'

As if by magic, a handful of stars suddenly lit up above them.

'I often wonder where they go in the daytime,' Bumblebee said. 'Do you think they sleep when we are busy? How can they sleep when the sun shines and everything is so bright?'

'Hedgehog manages,' Goat said. 'I guess some like the night hours better than the daytime, and the Stars need the darkness to be seen. Owl says they like to do everything the other way round.'

'Sometimes, when I look up at the sky, I feel so little,' Bumblebee said. 'I'm busy all the time. You know I'm not the lazy kind, but often I feel so small and insignificant. There's so much out there. What does it all mean? What do I mean?'

'You wonder about your place in the world?' Goat asked.

'Yes, that,' said Bumblebee, 'and also whether it really matters. Would anything change if I didn't go round the flowers every day?'

Goat frowned.

'But there's no one who knows so much about flowers as you do,' he said.

'Well, perhaps I know a little,' said Bumblebee, 'but there's so much more I don't know. There's so much that nobody knows.'

'Why does that trouble you?' Goat asked.

'I don't know,' Bumblebee said. 'I don't even know if it does.'

'Mmm,' said Goat. He needed a little time to think this through. It was evident that Bumblebee's mind had become entangled in not knowing things. What could he do to alleviate the situation?

'That feeling of apprehension that you mentioned…,' said Goat. 'Has it to do with all those things you don't know?'

'I don't know,' said Bumblebee. 'I suppose it could.'

'Mmm,' said Goat, 'perhaps you should look at things a little differently. Perhaps you should think yourself lucky. Someone once told me that a good question is worth more than a clever answer. If you were to know everything there is to know, there would be nothing left to discover. How dull would that be?'

Bumblebee wasn't sure what Goat was getting at.

'The things we don't know, we just don't know,' Goat continued. 'We can only fantasize about what we don't know, which, I think, can be a lot of fun. And sometimes we don't even know what we don't know, which can make life even more surprising and mysterious.'

'Are you saying that it's better to know nothing than to know everything?'

'I wouldn't go as far as that,' said Goat, 'but, yeah, new fields make dull grass tasty, as they say. The things I don't know tickle my imagination. For example, I don't know much about the Stars, other than that they're far away from here, and that they wink at me occasionally, and that makes it exciting. And I know very little about flowers — not like you do — and that's thrilling, too; just to imagine what you know and I don't, and that, maybe, one day I could learn about it.'

'Would you like to?'

'Absolutely, I would,' said Goat. 'It's always fun to learn new things, even though it leaves one with less things to imagine.'

'I'd be happy to teach you some basics,' Bumblebee offered.

'Really?' said Goat. 'That would be fantastic. But don't teach me everything.'

They agreed to have a session tomorrow. Bumblebee felt a lot better, knowing that she was in demand, that everything she knew was — for the moment, at least — more interesting than the things she didn't know. And, also, knowing that those other things, the things she didn't know, could be a promise, rather than a gap in her understanding; something to look forward to.

'Is there anything I could teach you in exchange?' Goat asked. 'Anything that I might know, but you don't?'

'I don't know,' said Bumblebee. 'Let me think about it.'

36   If You Say So

'One of the best things in the world,' Eagle explained, 'is rising air. Picture this; a sunny day in the middle of the summer, end of the afternoon, with just a little breeze in the air. The sun has been working hard all morning and everywhere in the valley there are invisible towers of vibrating, warm air. All I have to do is dive into one of those pillars of air, spread my wings, and simply float and dream away — all of my body carried aloft by the forces of nature. It's such a heavenly feeling; there is nothing better.'

'I have to take your word for it,' Cyrus said.

He felt a touch irritated by Eagle interrupting his afternoon nap with his lyrical outpouring.

'I'm doing my best to — as you say — picture it, but my personal experience doesn't reach quite that high.'

'Take it from me.' Eagle said, 'Nothing can match the wonder of being up there in the warm sky, circling high above the earth with not a care in the world. Nothing leaves you happier to be alive, more satisfied than to be so effortlessly elevated above all the comings and goings down below.'

'If you say so,' Cyrus replied, whilst at the same time trying to entangle the figure of eight that, during his sleep, he had accidentally got himself into. 'As I said, it's not something I can verify with first-hand experience, but I can believe it must be enjoyable. Perhaps you could take me up there sometime?'

He finally managed to sort himself out and looked up, but by that time Eagle had already flown away, looking for someone more appreciative to share her feelings of ecstasy with.

'Rude behaviour,' Cyrus grumbled, 'disappearing like that without saying goodbye.'

He rolled himself up and got back into a position that would allow him to doze off again.

But ten minutes later the heavy footsteps and thunderous laughs of Elephant, Bull and Hippo cut straight through any peace and quiet he might have hoped for.

'Watch where you're going,' he said. 'A little consideration for the rest of the world would be most welcome.'

'Cyrus!' they exclaimed as one.

'Long time no see, Cyrus,' Elephant said. 'We were just discussing mud. Don't you agree that mud is one of the best things ever? What can be more delicious than coating yourself in a thick layer of wet and dark mud, stamping and rolling around in a sweet-smelling pool of heavenly clay?'

Cyrus noticed that none of them bothered to apologise for crashing in on his afternoon.

'I'll take that at face value,' he said. 'It's comforting to hear that you all take delight in such simple pleasures.'

'Oh, but they are more than simple,' said Bull. 'Taking a mud bath is art in its highest form. It's like opera; performance, spectacle, sound and music, all in one. In fact, we're considering putting on a mud festival, to give everyone the chance to get a taste of it. Would you be up for that?'

'Not exactly my cup of tea,' Cyrus said. 'I'll pass, if you don't mind. I prefer something a little more civilised.

Please excuse me.'

He pushed himself back under his shrub, leaving the three mud-bottoms in no doubt that they should take themselves off.

Barely fifteen minutes later, Cyrus was once again denied the solitude he desired, this time by Bumblebee's bumbling and buzzing. Bumblebee was singing to herself, constantly. She probably didn't even know she was doing it.

'I'm trying to get some sleep here,' Cyrus shouted up to the buzz above his head.

'Oh, hello Cyrus,' Bumblebee said, 'I hadn't seen you there. What a wonderful hide-out you have chosen underneath these amazing flowers.'

There's another one who's forgotten how to apologise, Cyrus thought, but he was too polite to say anything.

'Don't you think the world would be a sad place without the vibrant colours and gorgeous smells of all its flowers?' said Bumblebee. 'These ones here are truly exceptional! Such sophisticated fragrances. I bet they bring you the sweetest dreams. You're so lucky to have these on your doorstep.'

'If you say so,' Cyrus said. What he really wanted to say was that he would feel a lot more lucky if he could finally be left in peace, but he bit his tongue and kept his feelings to himself.

'You probably won't mind me dealing with these beauties straight away,' Bumblebee said. She clearly didn't expect any form of protest and continued bumbling from one flower to the other, with hardly a pause in her buzzing.

'Be my guest,' Cyrus mumbled, too quietly for Bumblebee to hear, even if she had made the effort to listen. He slid back into his den. Flowers had never really been his thing.

Later that day, when the afternoon finally cooled down a little, Cyrus decided to go for a stroll. He loved this time of day, when the light changed and when, on a normal day, his whole being would have been perfectly recharged by his daytime sleep and contemplations. It was the time when he saw everything clearly, when he was always best able to summarise the twists and turns of life in one-liners that Aristotle or Cicero would have been proud off. But today, for obvious reasons, his head felt muzzy.

As he approached the river he heard talking on the waterside.

'I don't know what's wrong with Cyrus,' he heard Elephant say. 'He was so grumpy today.'

'I noticed that, too,' said Bumblebee. 'He seemed completely oblivious to the magic of the beautiful paradise where he lives.'

'Unable to appreciate other's delights,' Eagle butted in. 'It felt as if he put a downer on everything I said. Totally self-obsessed.'

Cyrus felt the anger rise within him, hearing them talk like this behind his back and with total disregard for what his needs or desires might be. But he couldn't just crash in on their gathering. He didn't want them to think that he had been listening to their chitchat but, equally, he didn't want to let them get away with their disrespectful gossip.

He waited a little while, until their conversation had moved away from him — long enough for them not to suspect that he had heard every word concerning him. Then he strode onto the scene, charm personified, with a generous smile on his face.

'Evening all,' he said. 'Hasn't it been a splendid day? Truly inspirational! So much wonder in the world! And for all that to be followed with this dusk, so suited to reflection and introspection. As the saying goes: *'The selfish fool, sees only himself in a shallow pool, and not the stars at night, that shine a brighter light.'* Beautiful saying, that. But ah, forgive me, I didn't mean to interrupt your peaceful evening so rudely.'

With that Cyrus left them to themselves, slightly baffled perhaps, but he satisfied to have got them thinking.

37 Could the Opposite be True?

'Moth, may I ask a question?' Dragonfly said. 'Where do your poems come from?'

'Oh, well,' Moth said, 'they come from here, there and everywhere, I suppose. Sometimes I go looking for them, other times they come looking for me.'

'What I meant was,' Dragonfly tried again, 'how do you decide what to write about? Your poems are always so beautiful, so well written and, well, poetic, I suppose. How do you do that? How can you make that happen?'

For a moment Moth wondered if Dragonfly was considering following a similar career path and, if that was the case, whether he should warmly encourage his friend's creative ambitions or, rather, protect his own patiently nurtured talent and not give away his rhyming secrets too easily to a potential competitor. But no, even if Dragonfly planned to follow in his footsteps, there would always remain enough difference in their creative identities. He could speak freely.

'Thank you,' he said. 'It's lovely to hear that you like what I do. In answer to your questions, I believe that careful observation is the key to all art, whether it's writing or making pictures. Did you happen to hear Heron speak about it, by any chance? I thought that what he said was spot on. Look around you, and learn! Essential, however, is that you look with an open mind. You shouldn't try to give everything a name or look too hard for explanations. It's enough to simply register things and wait until they explain themselves. You must be the eyes that see, the ears that hear, the nose that smells, and then you must wait for poems to happen.

If you're a poet, you can be certain that they will come knocking on your door.'

'Is that when you have inspiration?'

'Exactly,' Moth said. 'Inspiration is always around, but you have to show it where you live, that you're ready for it, that the fire is burning and that you have pen and paper ready. You have to get yourself into position, as it were.'

'And how do you that, being ready?'

'Let me think how best to explain that,' said Moth. He felt somewhat overwhelmed by Dragonfly's persistent questioning.

'I guess it's like going on a journey; you choose the right clothes for travelling, you sort out your itinerary and you take a suitcase. But — and this is important — rather than stuffing your case with all things you probably won't use or wear, you leave it empty. An empty case to collect all the adventures and observations that may want to be poems. The only thing you should put into the suitcase is your notebook, and a pen or pencil, of course.'

Moth could see that Dragonfly tried to imagine it. Was she picturing herself, he wondered, or him, Moth, the poet she seemed to be interviewing.

'And then what happens? When do the poems get words? Where do you find those?'

'In the dictionary, of course,' said Moth. 'That book has all the words that you will ever need.'

A silly response. He knew he had only said it to gain time for getting his mind, under fire from Dragonfly's relentless interrogation, back in order. It was a good question. Where did he get his words from?

'Joking apart,' he continued, just in time to stop Dragonfly thinking that he was stuck, 'it's a good question. Words are like colours, or spices, or beautiful flowers. I collect them on my travels, just like I collect what I hear and see. If I like them, I put them in that same suitcase, to be used at a later time, when I need them. The more you travel, the fuller your suitcase gets.'

Dragonfly wasn't done yet.

'It's so fascinating to hear you talk about all this,' she said. 'It's so clever. I would never be able to do something like that. So, when you have all those words, how do you choose which ones to use? When does the actual poem happen?'

Dragonfly's heartfelt compliments made Moth's energy and passion light up.

'Ah,' he said, 'that is where it becomes really interesting. You see, earlier I compared words to colours and smells, but, of course, words are thoughts as well. They mean things, just as we all mean things. In an interesting poem the thoughts of the words start shaping the thoughts within yourself, but not in the normal way — in a new way. Poems don't like your thoughts to be lazy. For a good poem you need to put roadblocks in the way of your thoughts, make yourself think in different patterns. Don't take the usual route. For example, you look at a tree and you see that its leaves are green in lots of different shades. But even though those are beautiful and useful observations, they are things we already know. So, then you turn things on their head, and you ask yourself: Could the opposite be true? Would it be possible that what looks green is really orange, or that the tree is not a tree but, for example, a fish or the ocean?'

As Moth heard himself speak, the image he had conjured up to give Dragonfly an idea of what he meant suddenly knocked on his door. He let it in.

'Listen to this, for example,' Moth said to Dragonfly.

Like Orange, like gold, like fish in the sea,
Like the waves and the wind, the leaves and the tree,
Like flowers and sunshine, like sugar and tea,
So soothing these words, for Dragonfly and me.

'That's beautiful,' Dragonfly said. 'Wow! Just like that!'

'Well,' Moth said, 'that's just an example, but thank you. Anyway, that's how it works. For me, at least.'

Later that night, back at home, Moth sat down at his writing desk. I'll write a proper poem for Dragonfly, he thought. She was so interested and appreciative. Perhaps, if I write something specially for her, she'll be inspired to have a go herself. I'm sure she could do it, if she tried.

Moth opened his suitcase, got his pen and paper ready, and waited for a while. But that evening no further poems came knocking on his door.

38   A new Beginning

'If you could start your life over again, would you do things differently?' Owl asked Crocs. 'Would you like a new beginning?'

They were both sheltering from the rain under the old oak tree, Owl on one of the lower branches underneath her home, Crocs with his back against the ancient bark of the oak's imposing trunk. It was a miserable day and — judging by the colour and thickness of the clouds — a reprieve was not yet on the cards.

'Mmm,' said Crocs, 'I need to think about that one. Why do you ask? Do you have regrets?'

'Not regrets as such,' Owl said. 'You know I'm happy enough — mostly. I don't have much to complain about. But I do wonder, sometimes, whether life would have turned out differently if I had made other choices early on.'

'Like what?' Crocs asked.

'For example, if I had read other books, or travelled more, made other friends.'

As soon as she said it, she knew that it wasn't the right thing to say, but it was too late to correct herself. Crocs had already picked up on it, fortunately with a smile.

'I take it you're not dissatisfied with the friends you have made?'

'Of course not,' Owl said, hastily. 'I'm sorry, that came out the wrong way. What I meant to say was that if, for example, I had travelled more, I could perhaps have met someone special, instead of living on my own with my books, as I do now. You know I love my friends, and I love my life. I have no desire for things to be different.

Yet, I'm still curious, now and again, how things would have been if they were not what they are now. If I had done things differently, turned left instead of right, got into sport instead of reading books. You know, those kinds of things.'

'Indeed, I do,' said Crocs. 'We all make choices, sometimes without even knowing it, and then we have to live with the consequences.'

'You don't have any regrets, do you?' Owl asked.

'On the contrary,' said Crocs. 'I think everything is perfect. Like you, I'm conscious that there could have been a different story for me out there, but it can hardly have been better than this one. I've made lots of choices and lots of them were mistakes, but that's part of the fun. That's how we learn, isn't it?'

'Absolutely!' said Owl. 'No progress without failure. That's how it works.'

Crocs laughed out loud.

'First you suggest I'm not the friend you would have liked, and now you're calling me a failure,' he teased.

'Absolutely,' Owl confirmed, playing along with Crocs' tease. 'We are all failures in some way or another, and all we can do is put up with ourselves and one another.'

They stared into the rain. There was still no change in sight, it seemed.

'If I were to start again,' Crocs said, after a while, 'I would try to learn more languages. Frog is brilliant with his Latin. I'm always envious of that. I wish I could be more fluent.'

'You're both very good with words,' said Owl. 'Frog may have the grammar, but you're no less of a linguist. You certainly know how to charm an audience.'

Crocs ignored Owl's compliment. All of a sudden, he looked a lot gloomier.

'Going back to what you said earlier,' he said, 'that life is all about the choices we make... The thing that I never understand is where destiny comes into it. Don't they say that everyone's life is written in the stars, that before we're even born our stories are already mapped out, up there?'

He gazed up to the sky, where, of course, no star was visible right now.

'Why then do we trouble ourselves at all with making choices, worrying over what is the best thing to do, how to get from A to B or from B to A, if at the end of the day we don't have a say in the matter anyway? If you really think about it, mistakes don't actually exist. It makes not a blind bit of difference what choices we make, because we're not in the driving seat.'

Owl was getting seriously concerned. Crocs' shoulders were now hunched, and he was staring at the mud in front of him. Owl wished she had never started this conversation, first almost insulting one of her best friends, and then leading him into what looked like a quickly deepening depression. She desperately tried to think of what she could say to make Crocs feel better, or, at least, turn this conversation around. Something perhaps about life stories, that things may be pre-determined in the stars but that it still matters how your story is told, or that you could try to trick destiny by unexpectedly taking a different turn.

But before Owl could make a start on the difficult task of pulling Crocs out of the quagmire, her friend lifted his head again and smiled, broadly.

'Ha, I think I had you there,' he said. 'Still teasing you, ha! You don't really think I will let the Stars decide where I go wrong, do you? No way! I'd rather make my own mistakes. Every day brings fresh opportunities to blunder! There's so much fun to be had. No one is taking that away from me.'

Crocs' boundless, mesmerizing smile overwhelmed not only Owl, but also the whole sky around them. Suddenly there was confusion up there. Clouds started drifting in different directions and a blue gap appeared. The sun noticed it immediately and cast a ray through it, projecting a glorious twinkle on Crocs' delighted face.

'New beginnings,' he said. 'As far as I'm concerned, every day is a new beginning. Lots of choices to be made, rightly or wrongly. We mustn't let a minute go to waste.'

He got up, nodded to his friend, and walked away, whistling a tune.

The afternoon brightened up quickly. Owl smiled. She knew that she could never wish for a better friend.

39   Upside Down

One day Worm wanted to see what the world would look like upside down. He was so used to always looking at the unfathomable depth of the earth in front of him as he went down and knowing that the sky was somewhere above him as he wriggled himself back to the surface. What would happen, he wondered, if he did everything topsy-turvy. He decided to have a go, there and then.

Finding his way down with his tail end leading the way was not easy. With his eyes now coming last, he didn't automatically see the smoothest passages, so he had to feel around for them instead. But there were also clear benefits. He felt more light-headed, relieved not to be continually facing the darkness and, somehow, remaining more closely connected to all his friends in the world above.

After half an hour he turned around to make the return journey, also in the reversed position. This was quicker, as by now his route was already defined, and facing the earth's core whilst leaving it behind was less mentally taxing.

Blackbird was surprised to see his friend reappear bottom-up above ground.

'What on earth are you doing?' he asked. 'I didn't recognise you, at first. I could have easily taken you for someone else and pecked you up.'

'But you know I live here, so you didn't — which I appreciate,' Worm said.

'So, what were you doing?' Blackbird asked again.

'Just an experiment,' Worm explained. 'I wanted to

know what living upside down is like. I asked myself, why do we always do everything in the same old familiar ways? What would the world be like if we approached it from another angle, if we made the familiar look new again?'

'And?'

'Interesting,' Worm said. 'Refreshing. I need to mull over the pros and cons, but on first impressions I would say it's worth doing more than once. Would you consider it?'

'Not quite my cup of tea,' Blackbird said. 'I like things as they are.'

Despite his personal reservations Blackbird couldn't resist telling others about Worm's avant-garde experiment and — very surprisingly, in Blackbird's opinion — there were quite a few who didn't think living upside down such a crazy idea. Very soon the fashionable new thinking rippled through the community and even started registering global impact.

Frog and Fish, for example, immediately saw the possibilities. Fish said that swimming on her back was easy and gave her the pleasure of seeing her air bubbles rise to the surface, whilst Frog thought that lying on his back would increase his capacity to stretch. Crocs said he was happy either way. It wouldn't make much difference to him, as he already spent much of his time in his deckchair, sunning his belly. But Hedgehog and Mole positively ran with the idea, said it was a stroke of genius, and that we should all do much more to shift boundaries and break through barriers. Bumblebee and Jay were cautious, but willing to give the new approach a try. Beetle was also positive and said the concept made him more amphibian, which was great, as long as he stayed close to a stick to help him get his feet back onto solid ground when he wanted.

To Blackbird's great relief there was also a camp of conservative minds, including Heron and Peacock (no surprise there!), who stated that the whole idea was ridiculous and not worth their faith or feathers. Ladybird, although less outspoken, also wasn't keen to sign up to the new movement.

Back at home Worm had continued his experiments, blissfully unaware of the stir his new thinking had caused, and of the division that was now running as a worrying split through the heart of the community. He had alternated his new upside-down method with the tried-and-tested way, honestly assessing factors such as ease of movement, overall enjoyment, general wear and tear. In the end he concluded that, on balance, his original way should remain the preferred option but could, on certain occasions, be successfully substituted with the new method to refresh experience and maintain motivation.

Just as he resurfaced with that conclusion, he found Owl and Bull waiting for him.

'We need your help,' Owl said. 'You need to put a stop to the mayhem you have started.'

'What mayhem is that?' Worm was honestly eager to find out.

'That new upside-down fashion,' Bull explained. 'Everyone is doing it now. It's chaos. Things are starting to fall apart.'

Worm realised he was being blamed for something for which, naturally, he couldn't take any responsibility. He had the right to live his life as he pleased, didn't he? What others chose to do or not wasn't up to him.

'None of my business,' he said. 'I have started no mayhem whatsoever. You'd better have a word with Blackbird.'

He popped back down underground, provokingly doing it upside down.

'What do we do now?' Bull said to Owl.

Both had, tactfully, not chosen sides in the whole new craze, more concerned to retain harmony than bothered about whether one lived upside down or not.

'Hope for the best, I guess,' Owl said. 'Fortunately, fashion tends to be a short-lived thing. All we can do is trust that, sooner or later, time will show us a sensible way forward.'

40   Being You

'Don't you think it is amazing?' said Bumblebee to Bull. 'I could have been born as anything. I could have been a bird or a snail, or even a whale. Just imagine! There are perhaps more than a thousand things I could have become, and out of all those possibilities I ended up being a bumblebee.'

'Do you mean to say you're not satisfied being who you are?' asked Bull

'No, that's not it,' said Bumblebee. 'I'm just wondering why I have become a bumblebee and not a bull, for example. I could have been you, you see, and you could have been me.'

'Would you like to be me?' asked Bull.

'No,' said Bumblebee, 'well, yes. I would like to know what it feels like to be you. Would you like to be me?'

'I'd love to, for a while,' said Bull. 'That would be fascinating.'

They remained silent, reflecting on the possibility of each being the other. Or of being Snail, who lived most of his life at night, or Whale, moving so gracefully through the endless ocean.

After some time, Bull asked:

'What's it like to fly?'

'It's wonderful,' said Bumblebee. 'The best thing about it is when you take off. One moment you have all your legs grounded on a leaf or a flower, and the next moment, with just a little effort, you are free in the air. Only the wind reminds you that you have a body. What surprises me, time and time again, is how quickly I can rise. If I really go for it, within seconds, the earth is nothing more than a miniature world, way below.'

'Is it cold up in the sky?' asked Bull.

'Not worth mentioning,' said Bumblebee. 'I have my vest, you see. It adapts to whatever the temperature is. But I prefer flying in the sunshine.'

'I like the sunshine too,' said Bull.

'Don't you ever get tired, standing on your legs for most of the day?' asked Bumblebee.

'No, why?' said Bull. 'As long as I keep my muscles in shape, tiredness doesn't come into it. I can always lie down of course, but life is better standing up. I can look out over the fields like that.'

'What do you look at?' said Bumblebee.

'Lots of things, really,' said Bull. 'There are always things that change. The clouds over the hill and the wind in the trees. The colour of the grass and the birds flying up and down from the hedges. And there are many dreams I can see on the horizon.'

'Dreams?' Bumblebee asked.

'Yes,' said Bull. 'I call them dreams. I suppose they're just things I imagine.'

'Like what?' said Bumblebee, 'if you don't mind me asking.'

'Not at all,' said Bull. 'For example, sometimes I imagine that I'm in a boat sailing over the waves, when all around me fish are jumping in and out of the water. And other times I imagine that I'm in a desert with mountains around me, where everything moves very slowly, as if there's no time at all. Those sorts of dreams. They only happen when I have been looking at the horizon for quite a long time.'

Bumblebee had gone quiet.

'That sounds beautiful,' she said, after a while.

'Yes, it really is,' confirmed Bull.

They had both become very thoughtful, aware that any further word or sound could disrupt the magical trance they had talked themselves into. In this way, they stayed together for a lot longer, until, finally, the sun disappeared over the hills.

Acknowledgements

I first wrote a number of fables in this collection some years ago, to provide story material for an illustration and lino printing workshop I facilitated for my friend and colleague, outstanding printmaker and artist Ruth Oaks, at Poole Printmakers in Dorset. Under pressure to provide 'content' quickly, I allowed my narrative thoughts to go whereever they would take me, whilst aiming to conjure up scenes and details that could inspire visual imagination. The animal story proved an excellent genre for writing fast, without too much concern for reality...

Throughout the centuries, following on from Aesop's Fables, stories featuring animals as characters have appeared at regular intervals and with clever narrative variations. My inspiration for writing a collection of fables was nourished not only by the medieval Dutch text 'Van den Vos Reynaerde' but also, since reading them in the 1980's, by the beautiful stories of Dutch author Toon Tellegen, in particular how these stories create new ways of looking at reality. I hope that, writing in English, I have found my own style of giving character and voice to my animal protagonists and their gentle reflections on the things that matter.

Big thanks to Carole Constable for reading and correcting the manuscript of these friendly fables, to Nic Vos de Wael for initial comments and, as always, to Helen Porter for corrections and her never-ending support and encouragement.

Petrus Ursem is the author of 'The Fortune of the Seventh Stone', 'The Truth Teller' and 'Black as Ink', the three books of the Steven Honest trilogy.

He was born in The Netherlands, the youngest son in a family of nine children. From his father he learned to play with words and turn them inside out. His mother taught him to listen and observe.

Petrus studied literature at the University of Utrecht, then worked as a writer in the world of education whilst studying fine art in The Hague. When he moved to Dorset in 1998 his creative work as a painter and printmaker took flight. Since his subsequent move to Cornwall in 2011 he started writing fiction.

Find out more about Petrus Ursem's books at
www.petrus-ursem.co.uk

and about his work as an artist (Peter Ursem) at
www.peterursem.co.uk